JOY IN OUR CAUSE

JOY IN OUR CAUSE

CAUSE

Short Stories

Carol Emshwiller

HARPER & ROW, PUBLISHERS
New York / Evanston / San Francisco
London

GRATEFUL ACKNOWLEDGEMENT IS MADE for permission to reprint excerpts from the following:

"Corn" by Bernadette Mayer, "Joe Brainard's Painting 'Bingo'" by Ron Padgett, "The Lace Curtains" by Lewis MacAdams, "Leave Cancelled" by Bill Berkson, "Talk" by John Perreault, "The Woman" by Frank Lima. From *An Anthology of New York Poets* edited by Ron Padgett and David Shapiro. Copyright 1970 by Random House. Published by Random House.

"Building a House" from *Where I Hang My Hat* by Dick Gallup. Copyright 1970 by Dick Gallup. Published by Harper & Row.

The Hero with a Thousand Faces by Joseph Campbell, Bollingen Series XVII. Copyright 1949 by Bollingen Foundation. Published by Princeton University Press.

"Poem" from *The Crystal Lithium* by James Schuyler. Copyright 1972 by Random House. Published by Random House.

"A Song of Autumn" from *Spring in This World of Poor Mutts* by Joseph Ceravolo. Copyright 1968 by Columbia University Press. Published by Columbia University Press.

FIRST EDITION

Designed by Gwendolyn O. England

Library of Congress Cataloging in Publication Data

Emshwiller, Carol.
  Joy in our cause.
  I. Title.
PZ4.E544Jo   [PS3555.M54]   813'.5'4   73-14310
ISBN 0-06-011234-4

Contents

The stories in this book first appeared in the publications listed below:
Bad Moon Rising (Harper & Row anthology edited by Thomas Disch):
"Strangers", *Cavalier*: "Chicken Icarus"; *Dangerous Visions* (Doubleday
anthology edited by Harlan Ellison): "Sex And/Or Mr. Morrison"; *Epoch*:
"I Love You"; *New Directions in Prose and Poetry*: "The Queen of Sleep";
New Worlds: "Methapyrilene Hydrochloride Sometimes Helps"; *Orbit*:
"Al," "Animal"; *Showcase*: "The Childhood of the Human Hero"; *Spectrum*:
The Richmond Review: "Peninsula"; *Transatlantic Review*: "Eohippus;"
"Yes, Virginia"; *Triquarterly*: "Lib".

Joy in Our Cause

The person you care about the most has just told you you're no good.

It rings true, but there's an element of surprise in it.

He has wonderful hands and always gives free advice even if he is, basically, a nonverbal person.

(These tears are just from yawning.)

"In Canada there's an island named Good Cheer."

Now he's laughing.

"Well, it's true and I can prove it because once a seaplane landed at the dock of our summer place and people got out and asked us where Good Cheer was and I didn't know what they meant. I thought they were asking for some whiskey. I never went there, but if I ever do go I'll say, 'I like the way you live, in the woods with your garden and your goats, and I'm quite dissatisfied with life as it is here on the mainland.'"

He's still laughing.

"I've never forgotten Good Cheer. Sometimes I think about it or someplace similar and take three or four deep breaths, noticing that I'm doing it because Ananta Marga said: 'Observe thyself,' and I'm trying to learn to do that."

Tomorrow we're going to a party at the museum. He won't

1

say anything significant, "You won't say anything significant," I say. "You never do." We go and he doesn't say anything significant and drinks a great deal. I'm unhappy about that because it will make him snore even more than usual. On the way home I tell him exactly what I think of him, mentioning a number of things I had promised myself I wouldn't, reassured as I was by his hand on my knee.

I relax myself finger by finger, joint by joint, starting with the right thumb. Ananta Marga had said to become a white kite on a golden thread and fly up to someplace of infinite beauty, peace and order. After some initial moments hovering, earthbound, in thunderheads, I suddenly found myself in a white place in space where all the stars were named by men and labeled A, B and C, etc., with dotted lines drawn between them and all the distances figured out and written down, everything mapped and the paths of planets and constellations drawn in circles and arcs, the giant protractors still in a corner of the sky. The gentle breeze of the universe blew through the stars and I was as white as space myself, naked and cool. This is the known universe, I was thinking, the place where the harmonies of the spheres are heard, octave, perfect fifth and third vibrating according to the laws of physics. And Ananta Marga said, "Return to your bodies but bring something of that place with you." It's the speed of time, I thought, and not the speed of light. Einstein was wrong, though he was a very nice man. It's the speed of time. How could he not have seen that? And we are here, set against a white background. It is meaningful to us. We have measured it. We are not confused.

Just then he turned toward me, his penis hard against my thigh (I don't mean Einstein), and even though I had just thought: We are not confused, I had the feeling of panic that you get sometimes when you're out on a dark hill looking up at the stars and there are so many of them they make you dizzy and you're afraid you're going to slip and fall off the world. Don't worry, I tell myself, you won't be called upon to do anything that any other living thing hasn't had to do at one time or another over the ages—lose a baby, lose a mother, drown or burn to death, divorce, rape. . . .

Yesterday I rescued a bird from the cat but it was too late. I saw it die, its tiny, pointed tongue sticking out, gasping or gagging. I said, "Do you know a bird has a tongue shaped just like its beak?" But Mother said my goal should always be compassion so I tell him, "All right. You can make love to me but sometimes the heart stops quite suddenly when you least expect it. Often, it is said, during lovemaking which is why, I suppose, we so often die in bed. It takes a certain amount of courage to begin. A measuring of priorities. Sometimes things work out pretty well when you least expect them to, but you never know until afterward if it was worth the risk."

(I'm glad I had compassion.)

I'll bet he's wondering why I went to bed and didn't get up for three days. (What was there to get up for?) Actually, I really don't know why I did it, but I think I was waiting for something to happen, something exciting or even just a little bit out of the ordinary. Not just any old thing. I wanted to be surprised! But on the third day I got up in time to make macaroni and cheese for supper, watched four hours of TV, made fairly satisfying love that night (I pretended it was Einstein), and I've been getting up regularly ever since though not very early.

But all I ever really wanted was a little privacy. (He says he's trying to think of ways for me to get it.)

"If movies are an art form," I tell him, "and I'm not saying that they're not, but then surely D. W. Griffith does not belong to their past."

"Does anybody ever really read those modern, experimental novels all the way to the end? Even Ronald Firbank?" (He's thinking he could give me a little corner of his studio, but I'm not interested in listening to that plan.)

I think we ought to read some books on love. Maybe one on touching and the best places to be kissed. One on little gestures of affection and when to make them. One on sex after forty. Books could change our lives. Let me read you where it says how often you should tell me that you care and the part about dinner out once a week.

I thought by now you'd have dedicated something to me, your companion of twenty years, but, of course, it's too late, now that I've mentioned it.

THAT AFTERNOON

Trying to work together on a common project, he calls me destructive to his creative instincts.

"My growing individualism is bothering you."

"You're so sincere when you're angry."

"I have what I think of you on the tip of my tongue, but I wouldn't say it."

I bend his middle finger back as hard as I can and he kicks me in the crotch before I can get away, but women don't hurt there as much as men do.

Standing with my back to the person I care about the most, I hide my face and think that maybe it's all just the usual isolation of the artist. We are making attempts, that is, at an alienation common to our era and to our generation.

"Sorry," he says, "but I'm breaking with society in order to get an unbiased view of it."

"I already did that."

The person you care about the most has just walked out the door and said a dirty word. Be of Good Cheer, I tell myself. Be of Good Cheer. Worship the sun a few times in a series of gestures stretching the spine and end with a little rest in the swan position. Think of Einstein, that gentle little man. It's calming.

Good Cheer is an animal, a small brown dog belonging to a friend, or perhaps it's a hot toddy. It's a pollution-free detergent in a green box with leaves printed on it, a postcoital sensation, an attitude that can be cultivated, a breakfast cereal.

They live like Indians out on that island, wild blueberries, wild rice, no telephone, no clocks but the sun, no calendar but the moon and the stars.

Here clocks are ticking all day long and even astronomers tell the time by their watches. Here people are dying as they breathe in and one of these days they'll all be sorry for the way they've been acting. (I've been trying to be mature, but I don't want to be the *only* mature person around here.)

Criticism? laziness? sloth? lassitude? madness? empty threats of divorce? imagined lovers? Shall I use *all* my woman-weapons if he's thinking of exerting his greater physical strength or economic independence? (I'm not in the mood for suicide, though that may be the biggest weapon I've got.)

But can I start some massive program of self-improvement before this evening? Hairdo, new clothes, laugh a lot and talk less? (All my life I've wanted to be somebody a little different, anyway.) I'm afraid it will take time, though I can reward myself with little snacks of things I like a lot like asparagus with hollandaise sauce or artichokes or frozen lemon crumb-crust pie. (If only I didn't have to cook them all myself.) I'll practice the new me in front of guests. I kind of like some of them, the guests. One has a soft, soft voice but I'm afraid he, too, may be practicing his new personality on me and is really not a gentle person at all. I'm afraid the gentleness is because of some violence in him and that maybe he has trained himself with electric shock to his balls or some other place just as tender and soft, so that we are both living a lie. Maybe I'm drawn to him because of that or that his gray mustache reminds me of Einstein. But anyway, I think I will tell him about Good Cheer and about Ananta Marga and her techniques for relaxation, all the while watching the person I care about the most.

I'll tell him what I think of him later on, like: "When I come across you suddenly in the dark corners of the house, I scream inwardly and head for an unoccupied room."

TV

I would let my life be televised. I would let them find out all about me. They could follow me into the shower and find out that I have small, (fairly) pendulous breasts, and I'd be walking around in my underwear or my torn nightgown or nothing at all, just as I usually do. I wouldn't care. I'd shout like I did today. I'd throw sneakers at the cameraman. I wouldn't care who saw it. My voice would get strident and harsh, my neck would get stringy, but that's O.K.

SEX

There's a woman who took a whole movie just of vulvas, one after the other, big ones, small ones, and from pink to red to purple-colored ones. Ten or fifteen minutes' worth of them. I would let my vulva be televised.

ART

I would let my vulva be televised!
(If you think that's not hard to say, try it.)
I tell the world that—I, who am not an exhibitionist, in fact who am the opposite of an exhibitionist (I can't stand being looked at), I, who am shy, and who feel uncomfortable if called attention to in any way, but who will do (almost) anything for Art's sake (though not for life's sake, so don't ask me).
But Art comes from deep within hidden recesses like vulvas. From secret feelings.
Well, that's only one kind of Art.
My kind?
No. Not anymore, or only partly. Yours has some confessions hard to make, but of a fairly "cool" kind. Besides, we no longer feel anything much when confessing things these days, whether

6

it's wanting to love a father or a mother, son or daughter, or just masturbation, and since nothing sexual is sacred or secret any longer, what's to confess? and we are forgiven (our humanity?) instantly by every aware person.

Aren't there any confessions you can make anymore? Has everything of that nature become too easy? Is reality so acceptable?

Reality is not only completely acceptable, it's very abstract once you look around and listen to what's happening. Reality, actually, doesn't have much form.

But what kind of realism are you after now that the deep, hidden recesses of the mind are so easily available as to be not worth bothering with?

Does anybody know what Art is or should be?

Do we try to redefine it every day of our lives?

Every other day?

Every now and then?

What will you give me if I succeed in redefining Art once and for all?

Well, then, must we do our Art without knowing any sure things about it?

Yes.

MORE ART

Newspaper reports bleak outlook for the Art scene. Less money for cultural events.

Let me tell you something about myself and Art. Art keeps me busy. Art keeps me happy at home (sort of) and alone . . . sort of happy at home and alone . . . alone and sort of happy (sometimes).

We really must learn to tell the difference between love and Art and love and hate if we can.

Art! We are saving our money for it. With our money we will buy the things to make Art out of. We will try not to do anything that is not conducive to Art.

If we are overcome by Art, as we are sometimes, and left leaning over with our head in our hands, our elbows on our knees, and nothing left to rely on; if we are left sexually aroused by Art for Art's sake instead of sex for sex's sake nor love, either; if we consume ourselves with desire for Art every day of our lives, living according to Art and from Art yet hardly knowing what it is, then we are living with Art as we are living with our love, head in hands, back turned. . . .

After the Art experience, take a little rest.
Eat something.

LOVE

I love him. I love him not. I love him. I love him not. I love him. I love him not. I love him. I love him not. I love him. I love him not. I love him. I love him not. I love him.

My face is aging. I'm becoming like fine old leather, smooth and soft and worn. I think I will last a long time. I'm wondering if he will want to live with me to the very end. Shall we grow old and infirm together?

When I married him I had no idea he was going to be the sort of person who gets up so early in the morning.

The person you care about the most comes back.

LATER THAT AFTERNOON

Trying again to work together on a common project, he calls me destructive to his creative instincts.

"Yours are outmoded moralities."

"My concept of eternity is different from yours."

"You said we'd be artists together but it hasn't been like that."

"There are some things I'll never forgive and forget. Once I read a book on being passionate and you wouldn't read it. Once you slammed the door on my hand. I bumped my nose on your forehead. Your toe is on my knee. This is one of your hairs I have stuck in my mouth."

(I must have married him for his looks more than anything else, though that doesn't seem logical.)

(I married him because he looked at me.)

"You'll never be an intellectual."

"Haven't you noticed my passionate love of truth?"

"My horoscope said I should avoid arguments."

"Do you still wish I was tall and had bigger breasts?"

(We are communicating on the deepest possible levels.)

(Are these the realities of a so-called happy marriage?)

(Oh, I forgot to mention our genuine feelings for each other.)

I'm watching him struggle with the problems of form and content. "What kind of realism are you after?"

Watching him and trying to shape him a little bit, wanting to lead him gently into an understanding of women, telling him about some of my own little idiosyncrasies, telling him women like gentler, tickly sex, even at the climax, that they can have two orgasms in succession, and some say even more, first clitoral and then vaginal. But it's all there in the books. I'm asking him to read one or two if he has some spare time.

"Are you trying for a physical or mental realism?"

If I have a chance this afternoon, I may wonder about the meaning of life or Art, or I may take time out to find myself.

(Is the world intolerable or *not?*)

We suffer every evening when there's no TV of the panic of being alive. (By "we" I refer to humanity at large.)

But I want somebody to love besides dogs, cats and children.

I put my left leg over your knee. You put your elbow on my shoulder (it hurts, but that's all right). We have come to no real conclusions as yet, but I take a secret look at your crotch and I see you take a secret look at mine. I try to imagine how you look without any clothes on even though I've seen you thousands of times. "Nobody's always nice," I say.

Good Cheer is a rock group. It's a look in your eyes.

The person you care about the most touches you possessively on the back of the neck.
I suppose I could put my hand out in some sort of caress.
"Say, did I tell you what I really think about Art yet?"

I have a dandy, fresh feeling of forgiveness, but it will take a certain amount of courage to say so.

The Queen of Sleep

This, the diary of lost sleep. New but not elegant. 3 × 5½. Green plastic cover. 365 pages. I ignore the months. Mark it into eight sections of forty-five days each, each section representing one hour of a normal night's eight-hour sleep. First section: August 31 to October 15. Second section: October 16 to November 29, etc. Five days left over at the end of the year.

Each day begins at 11 P.M. with sleep. Any sleep slept before eleven must be counted in the day before. I avoid fractions of an hour. Awkward to add up and unaesthetic if left over at the end of a forty-five-day section. Sleep must be timed carefully even if it means waking up earlier.

Every morning can be a renaissance, but why start with waking? Sleep can be a renaissance, too. Each of my days begins, then, with sleep and if only I could anticipate the exact instant when I drop off, or if I could count backward from five to one and be asleep, how much easier all this would be.

Signs to use in this book: O for sex, X for menstrual, √ for a happy day, and √√ for when three hours or more ahead on sleep.

Money: Pay myself a dollar for every hour of sleep over eight. Spend the money on those five last days of the year. Eat favorite foods. Go to favorite spots. See a movie. Dance.

But money isn't lost for sleeping less than eight hours because I will have lost enough already with the lost sleep. (And if I should stay good-tempered in spite of it all?)

Keep track of disposition. Take an APC pill. Exercise a half hour a day. Take a hot bath.

These sleep dollars will be more completely mine than any others I earn. One could say they are twice-earned dollars. They can be wasted. They can be squandered on two copies of the same thing: two *Marshlands* by Gide, two blue necklaces, or two presents for the same person, even three. That's why I'm celebrating August 31. New Year's Day for me. My little green book. But I wonder if the weather can be the cause of this sense of euphoria, or the moon, or perhaps the pituitary gland instead of the start of my year. (Do I dare to throw away my old notebook yet?)

Days are growing shorter. Nights are growing longer all over the top half of the world. By December even the Arabs wake up in the dark.

Waking on a bright November morning, I needed you. I have stayed up all night for you. I have waited, tense on my bed, while you didn't come. I have slept yesterday's sleep tomorrow and waked with a smile in spite of it and counted up my hours. I haven't paid myself a dollar for a week. New resolutions are useless. I write this letter:

Dear E.

I loved you again. I was in love with you all day. I felt it coming on yesterday. I was all warmth and dependence. Oh, why aren't you ever here at the right times! I could have been so nice. I could have been everything you've always wanted, anything you've wished for, but by the time you came back it was over. If only I hadn't waked up so early this morning, it all might have happened later.

Best wishes. (Dare I write, love?)

Love fades hour by hour. I think he has sucked at my ear lobe once too often.

The sick lie down, the dead lie down. People with headaches or sore feet. People making love (usually) lie down.

From the tightrope of sleep one can fall suddenly into wakefulness at any moment. From the table of sleep one can reach and touch the floors of reality with one finger or toe, because sleep, compared with death, is waking.

Love increases hour by hour and what I need now is somebody to tell things to. I've met the first-chair flute player of the symphony orchestra. I will tie my blouse up in front so my belly button shows, but what's his opinion of green capes and short hair? Those dresses with holes along the sides may help, but he can't practice while I'm eating and he'll have to keep quiet when I think about what my future course of action should be. And, thinking of that, I've written down the address of where you write to donate your eyes after you die (one of my possible contributions to society) but I'd rather do something entirely different. Give them a piece of my brain, the part that thinks about life in general, the core of myself as *femme moyenne sensuelle* if there is such a thing as a sensitive everywoman. Sometimes I doubt it, because if there is, who is she? Someone certainly untroubled by menstrual fluctuations (I allow myself an afternoon nap on my bad days of the month and this, added to the sleep hours, should put me ahead with my dollars).

Do they stare at me in my dress with the holes along the sides? I don't stop to wonder. It's the sort of thing I can think over later when I'm alone on the evenings when I wonder if my stomach sticks out. I can't hold it in more than a few minutes at a time but I've tried to whenever I was side view to anyone important. Do I eat too much?

The flute player might answer all my questions. I know I could do what *he* wants me to (if he would only tell me what he likes). I write:

Dear F. P.

I could love you if you looked at me while you were playing in the orchestra and I was sitting in the second row and this was Vivaldi night. I hope you will tell me what you want me to do. I'm prepared for anything.

Best wishes. (Dare I write, love?)

New signs to use in this book: & for a night spent listening for footsteps. * for sleeping all my sleep before 1 P.M. ∞ for infinity, as in infinite loveliness. Flute players have quick hands.

Things I like about flute players: Flute player noses, flute player lips. The strength of their little fingers. Breath on my neck. Sharp elbows. Black silk socks. I find flute players blowing into holes in beer cans and into the tops of Coke bottles or with pieces of grass between their thumbs. What I like about flute players is how they can say *u* umlaut.

I'm keeping all my resolutions after all. I'm coming out ahead on sleep. With my first twice-earned five dollars I will buy the flute player a present. It's for his sake I overslept this morning.

This euphoria has finally been identified as resulting from two cups of coffee in quick succession on an empty stomach. I suppose it's best just to ignore it. It may not last much longer anyway and what if I should find myself feeling unhappy right in the middle of some gay song?

I've met E. again and on the very shores where we first met five years ago and fell in love (sailboats in the distance, middle ground and foreground). He hasn't changed since my last letter. I mention flute players to him only in passing. I believe I have never been more logical than I am at this moment, twelve o'clock, Eastern Standard Time, the sun bouncing off my watch crystal and into his eyes. I have nothing to regret as yet, but I am plagued by an ever-present sense of *déjà vu*. It seems to me that we sat in a bar like this one at some other twelve o'clock with sirens down the street. Once I had a black purse just like this. Once, winding my Timex, I looked toward the reflection of the sun, wondering if I should offer to pay for my own drink. I could have heard the waves from here if I tried.

This is more than a question of preference. One makes choices on a deeper level than that. I judge the tilt of the cherry in my glass. The stem points to the door. On the other hand, the cherry itself lies with a wrinkle on the top that seems to be looking out the window (as he is). But I feel I have made this judgment once before. I chose the window which looks out onto the sea.

Sometimes I imagine myself with a knife in my back, chest crushed by the steering post, my hand in the blender, my foot on the third rail, drowning in a surf too strong for me. Perhaps it's lack of sleep that brings on such thoughts, but that's why I'm not listening to the sea now.

I sense the high point of the afternoon coming soon after the third cocktail, after he says, "I still love you," etc. I suppose it's always best not to argue too much. I'm agreeable but I'm not planning on losing any sleep. If depression should, in any case, result, I have a little pill that will restore the sense of well-being. (Now I lay me down to love.) In a dream I have seen two fish fly by. Will I meet him again on some other beach? I wonder, and will I think it has all happened sometime before?

But things go along about as well as could be expected and I will keep on with the diary of lost sleep just so long as nobody goes mad or dies or has a baby and if I don't cut my finger off whipping the cream.

Strangers

Across many miles of marshes to the west, below the wooded mountains to the north, lies the city.

The people have always lived: (*a*) on an island in the middle of the river or (*b*) on the outskirts of the city.

Skipping breakfast, they come out into the street, unlock cars and drive away.

These days it is said that the eye is the most spiritual of all the senses and touch the most primitive.

The people don't know whether the sea will cover their land or whether it will be the air (as they know it) that will disappear first.

Someone said the beaches don't smell like beaches anymore. That is possible.

We were the people in those days.
These were our ways.
This was our mass transit system, our means for the disposal of solid wastes, our endangered species, our Stravinsky, our abortion laws, our telephone company. We had lived this way

ourselves, sending our sludge to the sea, listening to music, paying bills, tolls, fines and taxes. We were crossing the oceans in less than eight hours.

Our mothers noticed that between the ages of five and twelve the penis hardly grows at all.

We miss the summer.

Instead of sunsets, we have the North Star.

Centuries passed. We didn't notice them except in our history books.

We have eaten the passenger pigeons.
Also the lobsters are almost gone.
Places vanish.
San Francisco might as well be just a name.

We've tried, but it seems we have lost the knack of miracles. We distinctly remember a pillar of fire or a fire ball on the mountain, but we were so small at the time we wonder if we only dreamed it.

Across many miles of marshes from the west came the stranger, having already asked us if we had once been the people, having asked us about the activities (cultural, political and educational) that went on in the city. He was dressed like one of us in a transparent shirt and fashionable tight pants even though he wasn't one of us.

"Have you indicated" (he had indicated) "the city and province of your birth in the proper place on the proper form?"

"Are you familiar with some of our newer forms of behavior, especially as regards sex, love and marriage?"

"You may have already won ten thousand dollars in cash prizes and other surprises."

Across many miles of marshes came another stranger out of the west, this time a woman, having filled out the proper forms, etc., and wearing a transparent shirt.

Art is thought of as life, or almost, and life as art, so the strangers play themselves.

Under their gaze we turn away our eyes.

We read odd things in our newspapers.

Our birds are dying.

Ceremonially we planted a small tree.

We have neither elephant- nor dog-headed gods, but we have chemicals that can eliminate odors twenty-four hours a day.

As luck would have it, we come across as civilized.

The city commissioner said that our women might be: muse, goddess, earth mother or whore, nothing less nor nothing more.
We have lived through all this before.
There are still places to go for a quick abortion. There are still lotteries. There are still enemies of the people. Some women still have babies, others still go to psychologists. They are the mystics. Some of us have regained consciousness on the brink of disaster and expressed our views.

In another era we might have said that one stranger had the head of an elephant and the other the head of a dog, but by now we know better. We are not deceived by appearances and we have learned to live with our doubts, so that if one has the head of an elephant (which might be true) and the other, etc., we do not notice it.

Our city commissioner said that a woman might become president of the country, but not president of the company (as General Motors).

We have heard about a great sage who grew an orange tree from the palm of his hand but we have not believed it (or we have felt there was certainly some entirely different explanation).

We have heard about angels of destruction and horses that count to ten, people with lion bodies and heads of men. We have not believed them.

But some things we have seen with our own eyes or at least on TV, such as a pole vaulter who jumped eighteen feet, and then one of us has held his breath for six minutes, twenty-nine and eight-tenths seconds. There was one of us buried for thirty-one days with his food passed down to him through a three-inch tube, and even here in our own country some of us have burned ourselves alive in protest of something.

QUESTIONS FOR A THIRD STRANGER

Have you indicated the type of disaster at the top of the page? Have you mentioned the time at which it will take place and the exact point where it will occur? Have you shown the dimensions of the disaster? The extent and type of damage? Have you described the physical and mental anguish?

Civilization has meant a lot to us.

However, we have had a pretty good society, a pretty good cultural situation for a long time now. We have had some people with a lot of good ideas. We have had instances of selflessness. In general, we have tried to accept the lesser of two evils. Also we have had a lot of very nice animals, plants and insects, crickets, for instance, cicadas, whales, zinnias, pelicans, baboons, marigolds, grizzly bears, bobcats, ferrets, sparrows, daddy-longlegs, and so forth for quite some time now. Also some of us have already lived to the age of seventy-five or eighty. Others can boast that they have changed the entire course of human existence.

We form car pools, write letters, make out legal documents and write case histories. Some of us have had horoscopes drawn up and our handwriting analyzed.

We still do not believe in angels of destruction.

We have given the best years of our lives to the outskirts of the city.

Patiently we're waiting for a third stranger.

Are we in danger?

Autobiography

When Gertrude Stein came to Ann Arbor, my mother said that all she said was, a rose is a rose is a rose is a rose.

When Dylan Thomas came to Ann Arbor, my father said that he was a terrible man.

And that was how I was brought up.

June 1973. My mother is still alive.

I love mountains and forests, but I live near the sea in a very flat place. I like solitude. I live in crowds.

One day Menlo came to work with Ed to learn about films and he was very nice and the next day Joan came. She came to work, too, but she brought her guitar and sang songs all afternoon and nobody got any work done but that didn't matter except that Ron came the next day and played on Sue's guitar (he wasn't as good as Joan but he draws better than she does) and nobody got any work done that day, either. Bob and Emery and Caroline came and danced naked in the living room for Ed to take pictures of them. The black paper cyc made smudges on the wall and they're still there. We ate on the floor because the table was full of piles of things and I thought to myself that I wasn't going to get anything done this week except feed people (that turned out to be true) and I also thought about not getting anything done this summer because of taking a trip out West. I complained about it nicely when people were here and angrily when all the people left. Then Nam June called up about midnight and I was glad we hadn't started to make love. Ed got up at six to go off somewhere. I was asleep but I think he kissed me good-bye.

Most of my life is spent not writing.

I was ten. I was thirteen, eighteen, twenty-one. (That last was the year I cut my hair off and suddenly everyone noticed me.) I was twenty-eight, thirty, thirty-five, etc. Even my youngest brother must be thirty-five or so by now.

When I was ten I still wet my bed.

When I was two Charley was born and got the room next to Mother's with the big bay window. Charley got my white bed, too. Charley is my favorite brother. He is growing older and has left his second wife. He is the most romantic of my brothers, but the least happy. We went to see him in Binghamton not long ago, but we didn't go on up to Ithaca at that time.

They told me I had a vagina instead of a penis like Charley. They showed me a picture and told me where it was and I looked, but it wasn't there. I didn't tell them.

Mother put me on her lap and sang, "Baby's boat's a silver moon, sailing in the sky."

I was thirty-eight. I was forty.

Two lies about myself:
A. I have very black hair and a straight, aristocratic nose and I have the kind of long, pointed face I've always wanted.
B. I can dance.

A truth: I spent three years in France as a child. I peed into one of those big vats that they take out to spread urine on the fields. They called Charley *"américain, tête de chien,"* and threw stones at him.

I have dreamed that I was stuck headfirst down a hole and could see the sky up by my feet. I think that comes from being born upside down with the cord around your neck like all artists should be. I have dreamed I couldn't move and I panicked and tried to scream but I still couldn't move. I dreamed that I couldn't find the street I lived on, that I lost my keys, that I forgot the combination to my (high school) locker, I lost my ticket, I couldn't remember where I parked my car, I was lost in a strange city, I telephoned home over and over but no one ever answered, I caught sight of you hurrying by with a portfolio and I thought everything would be all right but I lost you in the crowds in the subway. I was glad when I woke up.

I suppose ours is a happy marriage, and there still are a lot of happy marriages: Mrs. Wallace loves George Wallace, I could see that. Mrs. Nixon loves Nixon. Mrs. Chisholm loves Chisholm. Mrs. Cassius Clay, ditto. Jean Ritchie loves George Pickow. Margaret Mead loves Mr. Bateson. Mrs. Seeger loves Pete Seeger, and with good reason. Mrs. Lester loves Julius Lester (and I would, too, if I had the chance).

Delight in me, husband, when you have time for it. Swing me up to catch hold of tree branches. Throw me over your shoulder, then let me fall gently into the grass without hurting myself. Twirl me around. Did you say I was to be your partner for life?

Happy birthday last month (April). "It'll do you good to be another year older," he said.
Did I mention forty-three and forty-five yet?

We were talking over our lack of religious conviction with our respective mothers-in-law if you call that talking it over. Once in a while we come to a meeting of minds, or rather, once in a while one sees that the other has human qualities that cannot be ignored. (Nick says it's the innocents that make the best audiences, but then there's not much sex in his dance.)

No, Mother, I won't bite my fingernails, I won't hunch my shoulders, I won't walk like a horse and I'll keep combing my hair and washing my neck, but Charley said girls were no good, anyway, no matter what they did. He kept saying it for four years, from ages nine to thirteen. You didn't contradict him, Dad. You didn't even say, "Well, now, they aren't really as bad as all that."

Back in those days I never talked to anyone on the way home from school because I wanted to dream my own daydreams. If anybody I knew came around I crossed the street and pretended I didn't see them so I could keep on thinking. First I was a cowboy in those thoughts and then I was a famous musician, first violinist of the Philadelphia Orchestra, or a pianist playing Chopin, a cellist, oboe player, bassoonist, sometimes Ezio Pinza singing the lowest notes. But I've changed a lot since then. I never daydream. And being a writer is the most exciting, most romantic thing I know of to be or do now, or being a poet. I still tremble every time I think of it, though actually I seem to belong mainly to the wives-and-children category.

(I'm thinking there must be some way to keep on writing after having lost faith in plot and in any manipulation of characters. Even the slice of life begins to look contrived. I think that instead maybe I will manipulate the rhythms, the style, the organization of paragraphs or the words, or maybe sometimes just deal with little bits of fun or little bits of reality.)

Mother played Chopin, but now she has arthritis.

For a long time I was powerless to resist: my father's opinions, marriage and having three children, the lure of music. I should mention that from the ages of twelve to twenty I practiced the violin four or five hours a day and went to orchestra every afternoon, but it was my brother Bob who got to be in the Philadelphia Orchestra.

Daddy held hands with Mommy. Once I saw him touch her breast.

I was thirteen when my breasts began to grow. Then I knew I really was a girl once and for all.

Her work (mine) represents a slow, almost unconscious break with conventional fiction. She was changing her mind one step at a time. She read Jarry.

One time that she (me) thinks was particularly successful was when she was trying to catch the little, quickly suppressed thought. "You see something," she said, "and you might think, wow, that looks phallic and then you may suppress it before you're aware of your own thought." She tried to catch herself in these thoughts before they were gone. Then, of course, there's the problem of finding a form for this sort of thing. Her story that most exemplifies this study is "The Queen of Sleep."

At the end of that story you'll find this paragraph:

But things go along about as well as could be expected and I will keep on with the diary of lost sleep just so long as nobody goes mad or dies or has a baby and if I don't cut my finger off whipping the cream.

She feels this contains something of her philosophy of writing at that time. In her stories nobody will go mad or die or have a baby, but they may cut their finger off whipping the cream and who's to say that that's not as important in a person's life as going mad? (Think of trying to type with it!)

She says: "What's the hardest thing to write (confess) and what's the most significant?" She says: "Is it more dramatic that my grandfather died trying to rescue his niece from drowning while my mother, eight years old then, stood on the banks of the river and watched, than that I've been in the menopause for two years already now and am wondering when it will end while my mother (that same little eight-year-old girl) went through it easily and happily and never felt better in her life? They're different kinds of reality and menopausal adventures we know very little about." (She says: "First I tried vitamin A, then vitamin E, then I had to resort to estrogen, but I cured myself, finally, with Paba.")

She says her stories have become progressively "cooler" in feeling as time goes on. That is because she has done away with the emotionally building line or flow in favor of a more dronelike form.

She says her stories frequently contain within them hints and clues of the theories by which they were written and why. They are often allegories for themselves. (Not this one, though.)

She says: "A story is not an entrance into a dream world. Avoid this with a style that isn't flowing."

She says: "Can you write a story like your favorite Vivaldi concerto? Can you write a story like a bird sounds? Can you write what you hear when you hold a paper cup up to your ear? No. And don't try. Stories are, if sounds at all, the sounds of words.

"Can you, on the other hand, write a story that looks like your mother, gray hair, fairly good figure, osteoporosis showing in her dowager's hump, varicose veins and all? Can you write a story that looks like a Robert Rauschenberg painting? (I wish I could.) Can you write what looks like half a loaf of your own homemade sesame seed bread on a green plate? No, because you have to write a story that looks like words on a piece of paper."

She says: "It's *all* science fiction."

She says: "Stories! I don't believe in them any more than I believe in pictures on the walls."

She says: "So far I have never, ever, written anything directly about my writing except this."

I went to a party for Jonas's new book about film. I got along well with his secretary, Marguerite something-or-other. Across the room Jonas made a motion to me and said something I couldn't hear. I think he was saying that I looked nice. Later, to reciprocate, I asked him if he had published a book of his poetry (but he hadn't except in Lithuania). He has a brown, wartish thing on the end of his nose.

I went to the opening of the women's film festival and that was nice except I was tired and had hurt my back.

Someone should write a history of women. Where were they when George Washington was at Valley Forge with their men? What was Mrs. Bach doing while Bach composed? But we know what the women were doing, and we know what I do most of the time. I keep busy.

Women, put your urine in a little jar for the doctor every six months. "Take off everything but your slip and your shoes." (I'm glad I remembered to wear a slip.) Underwear goes in bottom drawer where they keep tissues for you to wipe off with afterward, and that's how I spent last Tuesday morning. I keep busy.

Emery said he gets his pupils to take a pose that seems to have possibilities and then they have to make a dance based on that pose. I said, "Why, that's just how I write a lot of times. I improvise until I find a good beginning. Then I improvise along the suggestions in the beginning. I keep what fits and throw away the rest; nine-tenths of it, as a matter of fact. Then I improvise again along the lines of what I have so far and keep what seems to fit (and I like surprises) and throw away most of it and so on. Not in my biographical stories, though." I really didn't say all this to Emery. I only thought it after what he said.

I always wanted to be the one that picked up the guitar and sang "Candy Man" at a party. I wanted to be the one dancing with abandon. I wanted to be the one in the long purple velvet dress reading her own really good poetry. I wanted to be the one with the wonderful sense of humor (but I'm not even going to go out to buy a long purple velvet dress).

Also I would have liked to be the one that married six times and had a child by each husband. I wish one husband had been a famous folk singer who played the banjo and we'd had music every night and one of his friends had come and played old-time fiddle and shown me how to do it, too. And I'd like one of them to have been the publisher of a good poetry magazine and have published some of my things, and one would have sung bass, one would have written novels, one would have been a guru and taken me to India and maybe one would be the husband I have now.

If you come in the house now, you'll see me as I really am, unkempt. I wipe my hands on these jeans. Somebody's old used Band-Aids are in the bathtub, unread newspapers piling up, also old mail, and I'm just sitting here on the bed talking to children, reading to them about the pygmies or some prose poems one page long, my favorites. They are scattering papers about. Their shoes are in the doorway. Their dirty socks under the couch. I keep saying it's not *my* job to pick them up and besides, I'm already worn out from sitting here thinking.

My daughter wants a goat.

As a mother, I have served longer than I expected.

Once a doctor said I'd be 80 percent normal after my back operation. "Guess what, dear, I'll be 80 percent normal!" It's hard to know what 80 percent normal feels like, but I guess that's what I am.

I was forty-six. I was forty-eight, etc., etc. I'll be fifty-five, sixty-two, sixty-eight if nothing unforeseen happens and maybe still walking around in the woods if I can be near a woods sometimes.

If there's a sunset over Brooklyn, we must take beauty where we find it.

Mother wants me to write something nice she can show her friends.

Lib

Jack is fed up.

Good-bye, Jack.

Wave to him.

Out he goes. Old black sweater off into the twilight and that's all there is of Jack.

Lib, in molded rubber shoes with air holes in them, thinks: Gregory, Gerard, Harold, Hilary, Ralph. She waves from an upstairs window with an orange Kleenex. "Bye-bye."

"Jack is fed up," she says. "Maybe he is going to San Francisco."

Maybe not.

And so she has gone down to a place on the corner of Avenue A or B, gone down where they sing at night to think about a poem. She has gone down in Jack's plastic raincoat with rain down the back of her neck and taking big steps like Jack does to sit rocking back and forth and the music aggravates an already too vivid emotionality with bump, bump, bump, bump, bump, bump, bump, bump, bump, bump, bump, bump, bump, bump. She would like to dance and swing her arms around. She is thinking: Gregory,

Gerard, Harold, Hilary, Ralph. She is drinking a daiquiri when someone puts a chair leg on the middle toes of her left foot and sits down.

Oh, sometimes it's daylight till after nine and people walk holding hands not going anywhere. That's what Lib remembers about last summer, holding hands, not going anywhere and seeing yellow flowers. Seeing yellow flowers, she is reminded of her mother. Sometimes she remembers her in some characteristic pose. Sometimes she remembers a characteristic saying.

Mr. Perlou, though not much taller than Lib, weighs a hundred and eighty-two pounds and not all fat but some muscle. It's likely he would have asked her to dance eventually but now she thinks one or two toes must be broken. She thinks how she lives on the top floor, which means five flights to climb. Thinks how she waved to Jack from the top-floor window with an orange Kleenex. Thinks: I have left a child up there alone. Mr. Perlou, hovering, nothing but a dark suit and a face to her. He isn't Gregory. He's a different man with the same name, one who wears a little dotted bow tie and gets up quickly and spills his beer on her skirt and down her ankles and down inside her molded rubber shoes and later on says, "I'm Gregory Perlou."

Oh, sometimes it's daylight till after nine and nobody's going anywhere. Everybody's small-town this time of year, nobody going anywhere, and Lib putting her hand over her mouth and squinting, having had too much to drink for the pain, leaning against Mr. Perlou's dark suit and smiling at the sky where, even though it's raining, it's not dark yet.

They have just passed a shop with yellow flowers. Everyone is looking at them. Lib, looked at by a man selling yellow flowers and by two other men and by a lady across the street and by four young men and another lady. Going down the next block, right foot, right foot, right foot getting tired now. Sometimes he carries her over the puddles or lifts her over the curb. The clouds are pink, all the neon signs turned on by now, and Mr. Perlou, only stumbling a little and giggling, has become, already, more than a dark suit and a round face, though he wears a dark suit and has a round face.

Right footing, right footing, Lib thinks this is an experience to be remembered but has forgotten the number of her new apartment, tries her key in doors along the way. She is wondering what he is giggling about unless, she thinks, he has had too much to drink as she has. Then I understand him very well and, with heartbeat in toe or toes, there is this wonderful rhythm to everything we do and a faint smell of beer. No wonder he's gay, and, in spite of what Mother says, does anyone still care where home is, does anyone care when it's almost always twilight and Jack has gone and there is this child waiting upstairs? Still, try the key in the door and it finally fits. Stairs look steeper than usual. Mr. Perlou wipes his forehead with a blue-rimmed handkerchief and then blows his nose on it. Now they must go up. "In a wife I would desire what in whores is always found," he quotes. She wonders, is he laughing at her?

Now they must go up, and she thinking: Is he laughing at me? Wondering: Does he know more than just this much so far? Has it been, perhaps, on purpose from the start? Chair on her toe? Rain? Man selling yellow flowers? Or is *she* the one who is guilty of it? Guilty of having Jack go and guilty enough to have put her foot under his chair? And would do it again in order to reach, at last, this state of one sort of almost perfection, going upstairs, dizzy, in Mr. Perlou's arms, head hanging back and down? Toe up? Pain? Beat of blood and smell of beer, and perhaps the neighbors looking down on her from their landings or peeking out from their doors?

And now they must go up. First he holds her under her arm and one hand at her waist. Standing under the light, she thinks: I, the one-legged acrobat of the stairway, holding my skirt down with my left hand and grabbing Mr. Perlou by the lapel with my right hand, the light shining on the guilty and I may have done it all on purpose. Instead of another drink, I could have said, "Excuse me." But I, too, must be smiling. It's the first eight steps up and now the hand at my waist has moved to just under my breast and we step on step nine and I think how often I used to take them two or even three at a time, loping upstairs, loping downstairs, so step nine, the beginning of my new view of the world, thinking: toe, toe or toes, and I have had an insight into the relationship of pain to life and pain to forward movement. I will remember this in my sleep sometimes, head hanging down, toes up, and when we have gone on farther, I will remember that on the first flight of stairs he had his hand at my waist.

Oh, even though it's daylight till after nine, the lights are on in the hall and not a single light bulb is burned out all the way upstairs. The wallpaper has yellow stripes and Lib looks out between the balusters from nine steps up, thinking: Gregory, Gerard, Harold, Hilary, Ralph, but Mr. Perlou isn't Gregory and has only put his fingers down the neck of her dress once so far. The wallpaper, reminding her of her mother, also reminds her of this very night. Lib remembering that she will remember this night and lights and Mr. Perlou, Lou, Lou. If you touch me, Lou, I will be the nipple under your finger, I, the leg against your knee, I, the tongue in your ear, thinking: As parrot to carrot, as motion to ocean, as position to fruition, so Lib to Mr. Perlou, Lib to Lou.

In the space between our faces one can put two fingers or one finger, but not three.

She thinks: I will say, "I was happy that day that Jack left and a chair crushed my middle toe or toes, and that morning I tried to write a poem," hoping for an insight, and now she has an insight but no poem or perhaps a poem, but all one can hope for is one insight a day. She is thinking: But art is not long. History is long. Art is as short as life and for our time. She is thinking: What if Lib and Lou lived together on the top floor? Looking out the window? Waving to each other? Upstairs? Downstairs? Raincoats in the hallways? And now, going upstairs almost as though it could have some meaning other than going upstairs, but not quite, and thinking: toe, toe or toes.

Now he lifts her by one breast and one knee. What if she were wearing an orange dress and a hat like a basket of flowers instead of these old things belonging to Jack? Sometimes unimportant things are important and already, from one or two toes, she has come to understand pain and its place in life, life like an earache as parrot to carrot, toes to heroes, as Lib to Lou and Lou to kangaroo.

They have passed a forest of balusters, a hundred yellow stripes and over forty steps, Lib not daring to take off her shoe, not till the top, people looking out and down at them and some people looking up at them now, at Lib, the guilty acrobat of the stairway under the lights like daylight or brighter and not a single bulb burned out all the way to the top and his hand is on her breast. "On your way up, are you?" "Yes." "Bad weather lately." "What will the weather be tomorrow, I wonder?"

Now the hand on her knee has moved to her thigh.

"Tell me all your secrets, Mr. Perlou," and, as see to secret, she tells him something intimate. "My mother was a very beautiful woman, wearing an orange dress and a hat that I could never wear, and so I have this sweat shirt that once belonged to a man named Jack, the little god of this staircase." "Listen, Mr. Perlou," she says, "this is my secret," and she blows into his ear. "You have quoted: 'In a wife I would desire what in whores is always found.' Well, I've tried, but no one has loved me and I'm still guilty of it. Not even . . ." thinks: Gregory, Gerard, Harold, Hilary, Ralph.

And if we should go down instead of up? Down the banister, head back, rain hat flying off, the pain in toe or toes maybe forgotten for a moment? And forgetting that a child waits upstairs? (Has it been left alone too long?)

At the fourth flight he lifts her by her breast and her crotch. Someone is practicing the flute on this floor and the flute player has the door open and watches them over his music stand while he plays unaccompanied Baroque. Actually they have heard the music since her key turned in the door. From the first step they have gone up in time to his toe-tapping.

"But *do* you have a wife, Mr. Perlou?" she asks. "Do you already have a wife? One that fits your requirements as you have quoted from William Blake, who also wrote about the little lamb?"

The flute player watches with disapproving eyes over his music stand as Mr. Perlou doesn't answer her question. He looks as though he doesn't believe her neck should be under Mr. Perlou's chin, nor her skirt up around her waist. She is wondering if everyone watching feels the same way.

What if they should go down? (But they continue to go up.) Everyone still out watching them under those lights as they go down (but they still go up). "Ah, going down now, we see." "Yes, going down for a change." "We see that even going down is difficult when someone has done something to their foot, though we don't know what it is. Unless, Mr. Perlou, you should put her on the banister." But still he could keep his grip on her breast and she her shoulder under his chin. They could go down the banister like that together, with her head hanging back and his other hand still at her crotch, sailing down, coasting down, gathering speed and swinging their legs out at the corners, having time to giggle again and then, for a moment at least, she would forget the pain, thinking: Gregory, Gerard, Harold, Hilary, Ralph, the beat of blood, the smell of beer, and perhaps the flute player would play faster and some of the light bulbs might be burned out by then, and what would there be to be guilty of, going down like big bugs making love as they fly and singing, "Oh, sometimes it's daylight till nine or later."

"Good-bye, everybody." Waving to them. Nothing but faces on the way down. Blurring out. "Good-bye." Get out the orange Kleenex. Wave. "Oh, we are fed up, too." "Bye-bye. Bye-bye."

But still they go up.

And the child is waiting, listening to them come.

Eohippus

What do I write on? Why, ordinary little five-and-ten-cent-store notebooks, like anyone else. Small ones. The same little notebooks a student might have or a housewife, say for lists of things to do that day. Right now mine also has a list as follows:

Eohippus   homunculus
peristalsis   nubilous & nubile
Watusi   pistillate & pestilence
God's thumb   philogyny
mesomorph   binary

There are two notations:

    A. Bags under the all-seeing eyes of God
       (as bags under the sun's eye)
    B. Check are Greek statues all uncircumcised

and a drawing.

I use an ordinary thirty-five-cent Scripto pencil. I prefer a red or a yellow. (I put this down for they say colors do have significance.) My writing isn't particularly neat. Someone other than myself would say that it looks immature and also petulant, and as though I were stubborn in places where one might better be easygoing. The periods, for instance, seem unnecessarily final. But I, myself, like to think of it as artistic with a sort of inherent pattern given to it by exactly that dark quality that makes it seem petulant. And isn't there something witty about it, too? the *l*'s so high-looped and sometimes carelessly crossed like *t*'s? the dots of the *i*'s exuberantly rightward? those nice little curls on final *e*'s and *s*'s?

Certainly I've always felt I would be famous. From my first memories, from that first feeling that I was *I* and that I had these particular parents and these particular brothers and sisters, and then later as I learned that I had these particular ancestors. You see, I was Scotch on my mother's side and German and French on my father's and when I thought that the LeDroits, the Charpentiers, the Kafries and the McMillans had all somehow combined to make *me*, I felt humility, pride and awe. And even during those difficult periods when it seemed there was nothing in one's whole world but rejection, all kinds of rejection, starting, perhaps, with the little brother in one's mother's arms instead of oneself, even in the very face of that brother, I knew. And even though I clung (as any ordinary person would) to faint, indefinite crumbs of praise, sometimes from years before, still I knew somewhere ahead of me was something better.

And so I've decided to title my Eohippus story: "I Thought I Would Be Famous by Last May." There is pathos in that. Of course, these things all change in the going over. They are all lost track of, so to speak, so that the original title never fits, nor any of the original first lines, but here is a beginning, I think, fraught with mystery and meaning. Something certainly to work from.

To begin then: "I Thought I Would Be Famous by Last May," and to continue:

I thought I would be loved by last May. I thought by then someone would camp on my doorstep, someone all trim with morning exercises and yet not young, no younger than I am (someone of uncertain age, one might say), but May came and went and I got a dishwashing machine, instead it seems Time is slipping past and now even the new dishwasher has a leak, not to mention the old appliances, what they have, and the car starting off in the morning makes speckles across the TV. The children are furious. And there's that dishwasher already making its leak, a little winding river across the asphalt tile. It takes exactly the same path every time, first a puddle six inches long and four inches wide, then, breaking the bounds of its surface tension at the far side, it trickles thinly to the edge of the wall and there another pool. It follows a law of flow. Here is nature in the raw, nature around just as it's always been. You don't get away from it even here. It's said: God is everywhere. Why, God, himself, said, or someone said it for him, "I am in the waters of the rivers . . ." and didn't he mention the stars, the mountains, deserts? and here He is, too, manifested in so many ways, right in my kitchen—voltage, wattage, cycles, circulators, agitators, aerators, tumblers, water levels, heat levels (high, medium and low) and my leak. (And He also said, "He that believeth on me, as the scripture hath said, out of his belly shall flow rivers of living water.")

But I'm looking for a lover, not the simple (complicated?) manifestations of nature in the raw, and can my hands caress white, baked-on enamel? Can one make love to electric plugs? (I've always known one *could* make love to massage machines.) However, for myself, I have always been, rather, a lover of horses.

Consider the horse, his naked eye, his withers. Consider, even, the lack of horses, the nonexistent clippity-clop along the streets. Clippity-clop, clippity-clop for centuries, but never, ever for us even when we were young. And yet horse lovers are still inauspiciously being brought into the world, star-crossed from the beginning.

But consider, I repeat . . . and especially the dappled gray, how he looks like a foggy morning in October, his a circumstantial existence defined by spots and dependent on the colors of the backgrounds against which he places himself. Consider his face, with twelve inches from eye to mouth, his nose velvety as genitals, and then consider I have always loved horses, I, one of those born loving them.

And the evenings *have* been foggy lately. For a week now there has been this soft, dry drizzle. Taking the garbage out, one expects fish flies. The air clip-clops. Gazing eastward, I almost see my dappled gray. I almost feel his lips upon my cheek.

Oh, I did think I would be loved by now, what with the nights so wet and warm (or famous).

Pause here.

It caught me quite by surprise, yet here is a stop like the Shakespearean couplet that brings the curtain down. I could say I did it on purpose and when I come to the next stop (surely I will come to another) I might mention, Second Act.

But to return to *I*. She has already a great many of my own characteristics. I have a feeling about horses, too, though I wouldn't say it goes as far as hers and I have had leaks in my kitchen.

That leak . . .

Hers . . . *I*'s, I mean. That leak, as *I* says:

That leak, as *I* says . . . sometimes it flows across the kitchen into the corner by the clothes drier. I think I could squeeze into that corner myself if I really wanted to, hug my knees and lean against the slippery white "appliance" on one side, wall on the other, with the 220-volt cord behind, vista of sink and dishwasher before, leak flowing from it to me.

And what would I be thinking of from there? Housewifery problems, I suppose, instead of love:

A. Daughter menstruating at nine instead of thirteen.

B. Four-year-old in glasses. Also his left foot turns in.

C. Neighbor says they took down her littlest's panties and looked.

"Goodness knows," she says, "what they'll do next."

One might well take to kitchen corners as smooth and comfortable as this one.

I see an impasse coming, Kafkaesque in its concentration on this burrowlike corner, *I* spending all her time ruminating in the kitchen. Where would it lead if one followed this tack? Certainly only into smaller and smaller holes. I would so much prefer to see *I* out in the dark of some Levittown looking for horses. Ought I to start over, I wonder, or back a ways?

"I remember Greek vases," *I* says.

I remember Greek vases with lovers of horses. I also remember Europa and Leda and some ancient (and suggestive) sculptures (no, quite specific, actually) but surely it is the horse that has God's phallus if ever there really is one at all. But here I am, rather than searching out horses on the streets of some Levittown, just thinking of corners in the kitchen . . .

What! Has *I* returned then, immediately, insisting on her corner?

. . . corners in the kitchen, husband off, progeny all in school except for one, unmindful of his mother.

Now there's a love . . . little body . . . I know all its ins and outs and I know he is perfection indefectible, sublime transscendence and most of all immaculate.

Also my thesaurus says: Paragon, nonesuch, flower, phoenix, Elysian field, consummate, Erewhonian, inerrable. Antonyms: He is not blemished, imperfect nor impure.

But what satisfaction can there be in him? He belongs so completely to himself, and if he loves me (he does) it's only because I'm his mother. He'd love me better fatter. He'd love me tossed on the garbage. He'd say, in his Boschish way, coming out of someone's bottom (his?) plunk in the toilet (but retrievable when needed).

Now the lover I have in mind is, except for pubic hair, as pure. Between his legs, nothing as cute as progeny's perhaps, but something to rejoice in nevertheless. (Can this be the river of "living water" flowing out from "he that believeth"? and is my faith great enough to find him?)

The man I'm thinking of is lank as a Watusi, existentialist, of course, an imagist, a Freudian distilled in Jung, philogynist and atheist. He sleeps naked even in winter and in his ears sometimes one seems to hear the sea.

But I love my husband, and more every year. There should be two words: *love* and *love*. *Love* for what I'm looking for and *love* for what we practice every day, he and I, inchworming toward some future where we can love each other properly and perfectly. But inches are too small. What there needs to be is some great dream-leap of love, by-passing resentments, selves and selfishnesses, demands, expectations and inordinate self-sacrifice. But leap or no, we'll never reach that *Love* love, though both of us are willing. That's why one wants a simpler love, more like fame.

But you ask: What has this got to do with horses? I might ask the same question of myself.

So let's see exactly what we have so far:

    dappled gray
    atheist god

clippity-clop
lovers
famousness
leak
I

We also might be said to have:

the LeDroits, Charpentiers, etc.
rejection
ordinary people
praise
Scripto pencils
and *me*

(And then there's a third *me*, too. Perhaps the most important of all.)

And now, since I've been thinking though not staring into space, we have:

But here I am, crossing and recrossing the same bridges, microcosmic archways, bridging myself, actually, when I might be out forging new patterns or perfecting my style. I might sit here devastated by my own imaginary emotions, brought on by situations pinned strongly to reality, as:

Dying of botulism from a can of tuna fish
Babies falling out of rear car windows at seventy mph
Crushed cats
Negroes murdering my whole family at midnight just
    because we're white. Me crying, "But I love all you black
    people," in vain

But taking myself in hand and remembering all my mottoes and such: *Write, Think, Élan, Fearlessness, "Étonne-Moi," Stay Loose, Jheronimus Bosch, Kenneth Koch, Petit À Petit l'oiseau fait son nid,* and:

I continue.

(By the way, *my* daughter hasn't menstruated yet and is still as breastless as a bird, but she's grown pubic hair, not at nine but at seven, and even the doctors can't tell why . . . why this enigmatic pubic hair.)

But to go on:

Now the dappledness of the dappled gray, might this mean black and white together? freedom up and down the land, all entirely solved at last upon the surface of this mottled, encompassing skin? (I'm convinced Eohippus himself must have been dappled.)

Then again, for this story at least, he might better mean nightmare, sea of dreams, the fear of death making us sweat at night, our dying eyes dappling the world with a black concentricity before we leave it altogether.

But that can't be, either, for I love him too much, though I know we are all supposed, in some ways, to love death. Is it really, after all, death's prick I'm looking for, so grand, so red? And if this is the case, what form would death come with to men? a tight constriction or a yawning hole ready to receive all of them, wetly, some Mare Imbrium, a dappled nightmare, then, of the moon, like fucking the yellow hole in the sky. It floats overhead from east to west. One could spend the whole night dying, east to west, that way.

It's three thousand miles or so more than what I'm looking for but I don't care. I'm satisfied. Or rather I'll be satisfied once I find it.

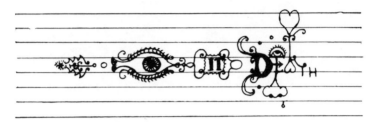

I'm beginning to think there's something to be said for corners after all. *I* must know, she must have felt by actual experience, how cool baked-on enamel can be, how smooth. Perhaps I'll not write: I thought I would be famous by . . . and not continue: I thought I would be loved . . . nor: Time is slipping past. (Perhaps I'll not write, either: What do I write on? Why, ordinary little five-and-ten . . .)

Oh, I still think I will be famous, for what about the LeDroits and the Charpentiers? and some of them really did come over pretty soon after the *Mayflower*. And all that rejection, rejection must have some meaning and some purpose. And I haven't been lazy (so very lazy).

But what I'm thinking now is: "Heard melodies are sweet, but those unheard are sweeter." Oh, those untold stories! . . . If mine could only ring in your ears like that!

Destinations, Premonitions
and the Nature of Anxiety

Fathers as teachers.
  Fathers as a good example.
  Fathers as examples too good to be ignored.
  Robust fathers of medium height.
  Generations of them. Dead men, pleased, on occasion, with their sons and sons' sons, but sometimes a funny little look around the corners of the mouth which, when viewed from the side, might seem as enigmatic as ever.
  How to teach the children? they are asking. How influence? Write a little *Clavierbüchlein* kind of thing. The *How To* book of life for ten-year-olds. But some sons die young.
  Fathers (as Johann Sebastian Bach did) (1685–1750) mark out the family tree in sons born to sons.
  Fathers let the wives name the daughters. They name the sons themselves.

  Whether fathers as teachers, whether fathers as a good example, robust fathers wearing glasses, fathers as distractions and distortions, etc., etc., are they to be denied and forgotten at the height of their own careers (or in spite of them)? I, then, one of a long, long line already, will be the father of nobody.

45

I must have misunderstood something he said.

I don't mind starting from New York City and only getting halfway, passed by thousands of cars newer than this one, having to stop and hitchhike the rest of the way or anything like that. I have this, as they said about me, "profound and incurable melancholy." Also cars run out of gas when I'm around. My friends run out of money. They misplace things, waste time. Pianists slam their fingers in doors. Soccer players break their toes. Trapeze artists lose their balance stepping off curbs. Actors stutter. But once I was voted "most likely to succeed."

And I don't mind being the eldest son of twenty children except if I have to be the best-loved and most talented and if my father votes me "most likely to succeed" and writes a *Clavierbüchlein* just for me.

I have thoughts of sons that die young or never are born, sons with eyes like my father's (blue, gray or brown), of a piercing and cruel innocence, single-minded eyes. *Their* melancholy is not incurable.

Bach, Bach,
Head like a rock.
If he's harmonizing,
Make him stop.

I'm passed by a station wagon with a baby in a playpen.
I'm passed by a man and lady arguing with gestures.
I'm passed by an old man with long hair in a '61 Ford. I can see he's one of us and I give him the sign.
I'm almost out of gas at the first Howard Johnson's.

First Howard Johnson's

Clam chowder, hot dogs, ice cream cones and coffee.
Has Tom O'Horgan ever eaten in Howard Johnson's? Has Bob

Rauschenberg? Jerome Rothenberg? Nikolais? Grotowski? Or do they bring their own sandwiches of homemade brown bread and Camembert?

How many lady research scientists eat at Howard Johnson's on the way to some yearly meeting of the American Council of Learned Societies? How many young musicians on the way to concerts at small colleges?

However, nobody here seems to notice how I look like Johann Sebastian.

"Pardon me, sir, but I'm the oldest son of that man who tempered the clavier by raising the thirds and lowering the sevenths and I'm on my way to Toronto to avoid the draft and I've run out of gas and I haven't any money."

WHAT MY MOTHER SAID ABOUT MY FATHER

"Take off your powdered wig, etc., Sebastian. Don't leave me here weeping in the back parlor knitting another baby's hat.

"One of these days I'll get sick when you're away and die before you get back." This is true. It happened.

WHAT MY MOTHER SAID ABOUT ME

"I don't want to be the mother of a man who doesn't understand women."

WHAT MY STEPMOTHER SAID ABOUT MY FATHER

"Sebastian, I love your bright blue, gray or brown eyes though you will go blind. I love the mystery of the second movement of the concerto for four harpsichords. When I hear you and your sons playing it I faint with pleasure and I feel like making love to you. Take off your knee breeches, your stockings, your buckled shoes, your Benjamin Franklin (1706–1790) costume, in other words. Let's go to bed early. Come and let me put my legs around your neck."

("When Bach takes possession of a certain rhythm, he does not let go . . ." says Wanda Landowska. Also, "Bach delights in multiple combinations of inversions.")

"But I can't help wondering sometimes if there isn't some other way of being feminine than this even in these times."

I'm passed by a car full of nuns.

I'm passed by a car with three old ladies in hats.

I'm passed by a car with the back full of musical instruments.

Passed by a car with kids who wave at me and shout, "Hello, Johann Sebastian Bach" or something similar. At least it sounded like that to me. (All us Bachs have sharp noses, square jaws, sensitive lips and a slightly German accent.)

Passed by four or five red Volkswagens, two from Michigan.

Passed by a well-dressed Negro family in a big white Olds from New Jersey. (I wrote a tune for race relations before I left this morning. Also a tune for peace, but my father never bothered with any of the wars around him. Maybe he was thinking: One of these days it's going to be two hundred years from now and more, and my oldest son is going to lose a lot of my manuscripts.)

I'm passed by a police car with two cops in cowboy hats.

There's that old man again in the '61 Ford.

Albany, Schenectady, Canajoharie . . .

All us Bachs are ectomorph.

FOURTH HOWARD JOHNSON'S

I see the old man's '61 Ford in the parking lot. (Dad, I think I loved you, too, but not in the same way you loved me.) I sit across the counter from him and give the sign. He may have long hair and maybe needs a bath, but basically he's a Concerned Citizen who won't even throw a candy wrapper out the car window. I tell him my name is Billy Bach (my father called me Friedy) and that I will be known as the son who lost his father's manuscripts, who cut them up and sold the signatures, who once signed his own name to one of his father's compositions. I tell him I will be known as the Bach who, as they said, "Gave up his post and lives without any position," "consumed by a profound and incurable melancholy," "dissolute" and all that word implies, but I tell him I did fairly well up to a point.

Herkimer, Utica, Oneida, Canastota . . .
A man goes by in a silver Phantom Rolls-Royce.
The radio (local cultural station) is playing Bach (J. S., though there really was a time when they would much rather play one of us younger Bachs or Haydn).
Deedle, deedle, deedle, deedle, deedle, deedle, deedle . . .

LETTER TO MY FATHER FROM A CONCERNED CITIZEN

Dear Mr. (J.S.) Bach:
A journey into the far reaches of sound is not enough these days. There are things of a much more pressing nature, more fundamental, more vital than music can ever be. Worry no longer about the conditions and qualities of the pipe organs in your environs. These are petty things. Persuade yourself to have a commitment to (at the very least) a clean environment. Also a concern for overcrowding. Overpopulation, of itself, causes pollution. One must advocate and practice birth control of every and any method in spite of some dangers, and, let me say here, twenty children is more than your share, even though only nine (among them one mentally deficient) survived past childhood. And you might have more consideration for your wives, of which you had two. Also, if you wanted to be fair to women, you might at least have listed the names of your daughters in your family tree and said whether they were musical or not.

Your name is a household word. Use your great influence for social causes. BACH FOR THE TWO-CHILD FAMILY. Write peace marches, fugues for black people, ecological scherzos, music to be danced to at the end of the war.

"Oobadoobadooba," Bach sings, and writes the beginning of a reply: "Most noble, steadfast, and most learned, also most wise sirs" (Bach really wrote this):

"The special and most gracious confidence of which your Honors have most kindly consented to give me evidence in the letter delivered to me makes it my duty not alone to express herewith my most humble obligation, but also to exert every effort to show by deeds how I make it my greatest pleasure, Most Noble and Most Wise Sirs, to show you herewith my devotion. But since this is an affair that cannot be set in motion at once . . ." etc. (Bach really did write this.)

The concerned citizen doesn't know why not and writes another letter about priorities, dates it March 1740 and warns Bach there are only 230 years till 1970.

WEIMAR

It snows in Weimar.
Bach in the snow?
Gray worsted cap?

It rains.
Bach walking in the rain, his umbrella isn't blown backward in the wind and he doesn't leave it in a corner trash basket because umbrellas weren't used in Germany until the mid-eighteenth century and at first they were considered effeminate.

Bach walking fast in the rain, in a hurry to compose the next concerto, comes home wet but doesn't change. Can't eat a banana (introduced in Germany about 1850) and asks not to be disturbed till supper. "I have to hurry up and, as they said, 'transcribe and enhance' something written by Vivaldi (which

I often did). This one will be for four claviers, the piano not being invented until 1728 and not improved until 1735 and not extensively used until much later. The early piano, by the way, sometimes had attachments to produce the sounds of bells and drums."

Bach in jail.

Wanting to leave the duke of Saxe-Weimar's service in order to take a better job. ". . . the quondam concertmeister and organist Bach was confined to the County Judge's place of detention for too stubbornly forcing the issue of his dismissal . . ."

We were fighting Indians then.

AREAS SETTLED IN NORTH AMERICA IN 1700
(When Bach was fifteen years old)
Areas more than doubled when he died in 1750

LEIPZIG

Here is Bach then (J. S.), waiting around for the renaissance of polyphony, wanting to be rediscovered by Mendelssohn in 1833 though he doesn't talk much about it, walking in the streets of Leipzig under linden trees in any kind of whether (it snows in

Leipzig), drinking linden and camomile tea for his headaches, aspirin not being used until 1893. Not much oobadooba, deedle, deedle, deedle in those later years except for you, Bach, your sons and Haydn (1732–1809), though unknowingly, having already become the precursors of the Romantic, but you, Bach, going on putting little black dots on lines, engraving your own plates sometimes, saying, "Well, I have this lifelong habit of hard work . . ." and saying, "Oobadooba, beedle dee oten dee, I have to get up early and write this secular cantata before I go blind and have an unsuccessful operation on my eyes in which the anesthetic used undermines my health to such an extent that I never recover from it."

Go on, sing now; you'll never live long enough to see a pin-striped suit or Niagara Falls. You'll never eat peanut butter or go through a revolving door. No Freud. No Chopin. No Picasso. No George Bernard Shaw. No instant replay, toilet paper, haiku or cowboy songs. No complete discography or disposable sanitary napkins (which only the unmarried women would need in those days, anyway). No Mexican sarapes. No Kleenex. No turtleneck sweaters.

Here is Bach, then, whose "dynamism is extraordinary," says Wanda Landowska, whose "gait vehement, yet not feverish," also she says, "he was counterpoint incarnate," in spite of the three wars in which Germany was involved during his lifetime, north with Sweden, west with Louis XIV (over Alsace-Lorraine), south with the Turks, but he, you, Bach, went on writing things like "Liebster Gott, wann werd' ich sterben?" and "Komm, du süsse Todesstunde," and you were busy burying more than half your children in, it can be presumed, the perfectly orthodox Lutheran fashion.

(He was examined by Dr. Jo. Schmid and Dr. Salomon Deyling in 1723 and found to be theologically sound.)

(He also promised that he would, "in order to preserve the good order in the Churches, so arrange the music that it shall not last too long. . . .")

52

Orthodox Lutheran.

Here is JOHANN SEBASTIAN BACH, then, 1685–1750
(Voltaire, 1694–1778; he saw the start of our revolution)

Children of Maria Barbara, Bach's first wife:

Catherina Dorothea	1708–1774	
Wilhelm Friedemann	1710–1784	
Johann Christoph	1713–1713	lived 0 days
and twin sister	" "	" "
Karl Philipp Emanuel	1714–1788	
Johann Gottfried Bernhard	1715–1739	
Leopold August	1718–1719	died age 1

Children of Anna Magdalena, Bach's second wife:

Christiane Sophie Henriette	1723–1726	died age 3
Gottfried Heinrich	1724–1763	feeble-minded
Christian Gottlieb	1725–1728	died age 3
Elisabeth Julianna Frederica	1726–1781	
Ernestus Andreas	1727–1727	lived 2 days
Regine Johanna	1728–1733	died age 6
Christiane Benedicta	1730–1730	lived 3 days
Christiane Dorothea	1731–1732	died age 1
Johann Christoph Friedrich	1732–1795	
Johann August Abraham	1733–1733	lived 1 day
Johann Christian	1735–1782	
Johanne Carolina	1737–1781	
Regine Susanna	1742–1809	

Is this any way to write a Saint Matthew passion!

George Washington was born in 1732.
He could have been one of Bach's younger sons. We might
have had more of a musical revolution if that had been the case.

Destinations, Premonitions and the Nature of Anxiety   53

Bach's youngest son, the so-called English Bach, was three years younger than George Washington and turned Catholic. (Powdered wigs were still in style.)

Haydn was also born in 1732.

Music, up to this time, is mostly two-part song form: AB, AB (as opposed to three-part song form: ABA), with mordents, trills, roulades, appoggiaturas. Much later they will compose things like the "Bell Song" from *Lakmé*.

Daddle ah ta, ta, ta, daddle ah dah . . .

"Sometimes we tire of the grandiose,"

             wrote Wanda Landowska. Also,

"and if we lack air

in the thick

      atmosphere

of exaggerated romanticism,

we need only

          to open

               wide

the windows . . ."

WHAT I SAID ABOUT MYSELF

I'm the eldest son of twenty children. I haven't yet taken to drink. Mother wants me to learn about music and women. (Also my stepmother.) She wanted to be the mother of a man who would know what to say when a woman needed an extra word of love. She wanted to be the mother of a man with a less tentative approach. She wanted to be the mother of a man who is inwardly composed, outwardly energetic, and well known in musical circles. She wanted to be the mother of a son who would have a son named Johann Sebastian.

My half sister had a little boy named Johann Sebastian Altnikol but he died within a year. None of my other sisters ever married, consumed, as they may also have been, by a "profound and incurable melancholy."

Auburn, Canandaigua, Rochester, Batavia, Buffalo . . .
If I have an accident at least it will be something.
I cross the Peace Bridge, but what's in a name?

Bach, Bach,
Hole in his sock,
If he's (insert one) rhapsodizing, memorizing, concertizing,
Make him stop.

SEVENTH HOWARD JOHNSON's (open the windows)

Clam chowder, hot dogs, ice cream cones and coffee.
A telephone line to the dead from here. Concerned Citizen calls
up Johann Sebastian Bach: "Hello. Is this Mr. Bach? We're glad
to have had you with us here on Earth for a little while."
Bach (J. S.): "I do have one more little thing to say to the audiences of the future still listening in thirds, sixths and octaves to
little slivers of music while many composers are making shapeless
and inexplicable sounds on instruments yet to be invented: well,
let them go on making funny noises."

REFERENCES

Landowska on Music. Collected, edited and translated by Denise
    Restout, assisted by Robert Hawkins. New York: Stein and Day,
    1969.
The Bach Reader. Edited by Hans David and Arthur Mendel.
    New York: Norton, 1966.
Bach. Eva and Sydney Grew. New York: Octagon, 1949.
The Encyclopaedia Britannica, and others.

To the Association

To the association of astronomers the Sixteenth of November is a person who has invented all the hours, one to twelve. I find him of a different sort, with meanings I have to look up in books: Xiuhtecuhtli or Chalchihuitlicue or Ixbalanqué or Tezcatlipoca.

I'm waiting on the banks of a river to find out more about these people who measure distances in hats.

However, the old Indian that *I* know of lives at the zoo (he has a Jewish nose, but Chinese eyes) and my little brother wrote down his language in ð, ɸ, ə and other symbols in exchange for a few string tricks. I don't yet know (personally) any other American Indians, but I belong to a committee that wants to find out more.

The Sixteenth of November, that inventor of hours, lives with the last of a certain kind of sparrow and he remembers how to chip obsidian and knows how the world began and what sort of ritual started it off. The association of astronomers has calculated his birth date and made plans to care for his simple needs. They have received a small grant from an educational foundation.

"I invented the hours of the day," he said, "and arranged them in their proper order."

The old man was seeking status of some sort.

"I am the eleventh month out of a possible thirteen.

"Six o'clock is the first hour," he told us, but we all knew that. We rewarded him for effort.

"Try again," we said.

(We studied his kind of art and incorporated it into our own.)

My little brother had shoes made for him by this old Indian and he learned a song about a tree, but he has forgotten it. "Tell me about your old Indian," I asked him once, but there wasn't much to say. Everyone had their own Indian at that place in Oklahoma. All the young men had old Indians to study. He learned a lot of string tricks. He remembers one or two of them.

"What is the meaning of these tricks with handmade strings?"

Once all the women lived underground in a different place. Then they came up and lived in huts in the forest, but they were homesick for the tunnels and chambers of their former life. They lost confidence in themselves regardless of race, age or class because of the uncertainty and unfamiliarity of the new place and they feared, above all, the trees. It seemed to them that the trees could assume the shapes of men in the darkness. Possibly, at that time, the hours had not yet been invented.

"Give us time," the women said, "to rehearse for life in this country and time also for our monthly celebrations of menstrual blood and to dance with our queen."

The Sixteenth of November gave them hours but still they had no confidence in themselves and no time for the celebrations of the menstrual and this was important to them.

"The old man is seeking status for himself," they said, and

laughed and turned away without confidence. "After all, he is only the eleventh month out of a possible thirteen."

But he was not angry with them because he understood how hard it was to come up out of the ground and live in a different place entirely and to be afraid of the trees which were all about them and he heard them going about calling the trees a necessary evil and everyone saying, "Give up your old way of life for new pleasures of a different sort," and he felt that the women did not need consecutive days, so he thought that he would not tell the women about them. None of the women ever heard about the consecutive days then and never had any time for their celebrations though there was no anger in not telling them about it. After a while the women found out about the days from their lovers but it didn't make any difference in their confidence. Even though they could calculate the time of the next menstrual and mark it with an X on that day, they still had no self-confidence.

On the sixteenth of November they held the world conference on improvements in rice, lentils and beans. The old man didn't attend. Perhaps he was already dead.

I feel sad.

I think I might tell the astronomers about other hours they never heard of and places where the days come in groups of three.

Well, that's all right because even in those places the children lose their baby teeth and bring them, one by one, to their mothers. The new teeth are the teeth of reasoning, including the judgment of distance, time and volume, and if the new teeth should, at some later date, fall out, that would be the time of the loss of time and understanding.

The astronomers know this by now. Some of them have already lived through the complete cycle and are coming to a very long time where they sit with the sun on their laps. All the women in their lives are dead and they are getting their own cups of tea. (They are giving their cast-off clothes to the Indians.)

We would rather not disturb them now, but we want to know a few things that they might have remembered, so another meeting of the astronomers has been scheduled in a different month. It's official. I mark an X on that day.

A person has many meanings but a man of the hour has only one. The astronomers have found that the same is true, in a way, for the sky. They are tired of counting the stars and of their distances. They would like to know things as the bees know them, by doing a little dance in a figure eight, and they would like to see in a circle like a fish.

My committee on the Indians is going to meet with their committee, not so much to think about the stars as the clouds, which we can all understand together. I hold hands with the oldest astronomer of all and we think about dancing in a figure eight but we don't do it. "The bees dance infinity," he says, "did you know that?" and at last I understand everything.

It's been a profitable three days.

In the time to knit a fairly long scarf, I have learned about the universe.

Biography of
an Uncircumcised Man
(Including Interview)

John is a poet.
  There are many kinds of poets.
  What kind of a poet is John?

John is an eager young poet, self-aware and interested in discovery. He believes that new awarenesses necessitate new forms
and even that new forms, of themselves, can generate new awarenesses. He is also the kind of poet who is trying out behaviorist
conditioning and Freudian analysis at the same time to see what
they feel like.
  Except for one little thing, John is a very sane poet.

  Poets look like everyone else.
  John looks like everyone else.

Once upon a time there was a young prince who was a poet.
The prince's name was John or Tom.
  The prince's name was really Ed and he was not a poet at all,
but a film maker who was not afraid of heights and with a certain
reputation among his own kind and he lived in a little house with

his wife and three children and made just enough money for his needs, even though film making is very expensive.

Coming in singing old songs one afternoon (like "Rock Around the Clock" and "Love and Marriage" and "The Music Goes Round and Round" and so forth) and after military service in Italy in 1945 and the University of Michigan Art School in 1947, getting a little fatter as he grows older, hair thinning, having had a beard since a Canadian summer in 1957, suitcase ready to take the first plane to Greensboro or Ithaca or Ann Arbor or some other college town, he made love to me (it came out about four on a scale of ten) and went to Chicago.

He isn't one of those husbands who recognize their wives at a glance.

"Ed, first lie close to me, your leg over my leg, and tickle my left breast with your tongue."

Poets say a lot of things everybody else says, even in their poems, like:

"So as I was saying to you
yesterday"   *John Perreault*

and: "A dog disappears
across a small lake"   *Joseph Ceravolo*

and: "I have nothing to write you except
I am feeling dizzy again"   *Lewis MacAdams*

and: "Suppose you had plenty money"
                                         James Schuyler

and: "I don't know anything about hemorrhoids"
                                           Ron Padgett

(Ron Padgett thinks about Frank O'Hara, but *I* think about Ron Padgett *and* Frank O'Hara.)

Here are four beginnings of poems:

"Returning from the movies we find"   *Dick Gallup*

"Corn is a small hard seed"   *Bernadette Mayer*

"Today I met my woman in the subway"   *Frank Lima*

"What we need is a great big vegetable farm!"
Bill Berkson

which illustrate the same point as above.
I like that.

I know a poet who has an eagle tattooed on his chest but I'm not going to say his name. (Tom D.) "Do you want to see my eagle?" he said.

"Of course," I said, and I was impressed.

(That was a strange thing for Tom to do. It may have been that it was the end of a love affair. I wonder what he thinks about it now.)

John the poet's mother is thin.
Tom's mother is dead.
Ed the film maker's mother is fat.
Ed is six feet tall and weighs 180 lbs.
Ed's mother is five feet three and weighs 155 lbs.
Ed's children, at their present stage and in spite of their varying ages (12, 14 and 15) are all about five feet four and weigh around 100 lbs.

Ed got first prize in 1959 for his first film and the year after that he got an honorable mention and that was good, too, and the year after that, something else, but after that they didn't give any more prizes at that place so he had to win prizes someplace else.

When he dies, I will reorganize Ed's attic workrooms into a pleasant bedroom/writing room for myself. I will paint the walls white and open the windows, which are now covered over with black plywood in order to be able to show movies there in the daytime. Or, instead, I may move out to some college town, Greensboro, Ithaca, or Ann Arbor. I was wondering if I could support myself writing confessions of sins I never even wanted to commit or adventure stories like the lives and loves of some of the poets I know (Tom D. or John H.).

But I expect it to take a year or two to get back to writing after his death.

John is an eager young poet, as I said, but Ed is not so young, forty-five or forty-six. Ed is an eager older film maker, perhaps not as self-aware as a poet would be, nor as verbal, perhaps a master of one sort of nonverbal expression, of whom it was written by Sheldon Renan:

Many people in the underground (film) can, in fact, get whatever they wish out of a camera. Stan Brakhage, Marie Menken and Ed . . .

If some of the underground film makers were arranged according to height, smallest first, they would line up like this:

Storm De Hirsch, by far the shortest
then Maya Deren
Willard Maas
Shirley Clark
Jonas Mekas
Adolphus Mekas
Gregory Markopoulos
Ken Jacobs
Ed

Marie Menken
Stan Vanderbeek
Hilary Harris

Five things Ed likes:

Steaks
Martinis
Having his back rubbed
Making movies
Playing the guru

When I asked him what five things he likes, Ed said:

Making movies
Me
The kids
Travel and having adventures
Learning something new

I know three poets whose names are all Bob.

I know a white poet who has a little Negro son.

I know Jack, who is a fairly small poet with dark hair and a sharp nose. His daughter is five years old and looks like him. His wife is pregnant. He's twenty-eight years old.

(Sometimes I think you can't really know who a person is until you see their wife, if any, and children.)

So . . .

Ed has:

One dark-haired, brown-eyed daughter, well built since she matured last year

One thin, awkward, blondish daughter with green/tan eyes

One blondish, tan-eyed, left-handed son who is large for his age

I am Ed's wife.

I know of a poet who had a wild surmise and another who wrote, as though he were a cloud, "I bring fresh showers . . ." and one who had strange fits of passion, but these were a long time ago.

Who is that small-sized poet sitting shyly on the stairs?
Who is the poet playing the piano?
Who is the poet in the blue farmer shirt?
Who is that tall, sweaty, hairy poet with the loud laugh?
That isn't a poet. That's Ed, the film maker.

Hail, Prince John, Tom D. (or Ed man of a lot of ideas, everyday morality and nice blue eyes)!

When they dug up Haydn to examine his brain, it was found to be not unlike the brains of all the rest of us.

Ed says: "I was born to the fat lady in the circus. My father was either the clown who jumps out of the burning house from the top floor or the giant with a pituitary problem." (Some of this is only a little bit true.) "I was conceived at the very hour of an early-morning disaster in which seventy-three senile people were burned to death. Most of my childhood was spent on a tightrope and with dwarfs my own size at any given time and this accounts for some of my personality hangups."

There's a season for people like Ed, but it's not spring.

Ed says: "I have this skin disease behind my ears or under my arms that makes me itch. I put some medicine on it but it doesn't do any good."

We read Van de Velde's marriage manual together and tried some of the positions.

Ed has a strange way of hunching his shoulders. I kind of like it.

Well, what *is* your favorite season of the year?

As we adjust to a poet or get to know him better or two or three poets or sometimes as many as sixteen poets at the same party, as we make adjustments to poets almost as though they were like anyone else, we must remember that they sometimes do amount to something and even may make a little money. (John has only put out one little book of poems so far. It costs two dollars for sixty pages.)

As a prince, how do you find life in a democracy of sorts? As a guru, how do you like making occasional mistakes? As an artist, you could draw me writing at the kitchen table like this or doing dishes or wiping cat throw-up off the rug. As a poet, you could do the lyrics to my tunes. As a film maker, do me walking in the woods.
You did that.

Japanese poets are nice.

Poets with addresses on Park Avenue. Poets from the ghetto. Poets in prison. Shoeshine poets of Chicago or Detroit. Radical poets. Black poets. Women's lib poets. Trying to tell you something. Telling everybody things. Are they (you) turning little everyday things into art? Have you (they) been thinking about reality lately? *Have you been thinking about reality!* What is the realest thing you do this time of year? Is this art? Do a real thing. Do not think about it. Now do an unreal thing. Do not think about it. Does it matter?
There are hidden realities.
There are pure and impure realities.

Some realities do not last long.

Can you call together a small group of eager young poets and tell them about this?

"Uh . . . ah . . . well . . . ww . . . uh . . ."

Your bloodshot eyes give me the creeps.

Your stomach sticks out.

You have a pimple on your shoulder.

"Remember, friends, nobody's perfect."

Ed says: "In my first film I wanted to combine a dancer with moving animated paintings." (He says that every time.) "In my second film I wanted to do pure abstractions, moving paintings that would arouse emotion in the viewers for no concrete reasons, abstract laughter, abstract tension. That sort of thing."

Anybody who's had their finger pinched in a door so badly that it split like a squashed grape has some awareness of the agonies of creativity.

Knowing this, I have always given him the best slice of roast beef, the butteriest piece of toast, the eggs with the yolks unbroken, the biggest apple.

Ed says: "The camera is a remarkable invention which my parents said I should buy a radio instead of, so during my formative years I had a radio. I got my own movie camera at the age of thirty or thereabouts."

I, too, have had a childhood full of frustrations.

"Where do you get all your good ideas?"

"Uh . . . ah . . . well . . . ww . . . uh . . ."

"To what do you owe . . ."

"Who me?"

". . . the cosmic

quality of your movies?"

INTERVIEW

ME: Uh . . . the questions are . . . uh . . . serious and some are sort of not and some are just asking questions and some are . . . I really mean for real answers

ED: So I should give you straight answers all the time, right?

ME: Well, yeah.

ED: . . . or whatever I feel like.

ME: Well, however you feel. It doesn't really matter.

ED: It's as I'm slowly getting plastered.

ME: What I mean is that it's not a . . . a serious . . . even the *serious* ones don't have to be serious . . . like that. You know what I mean. Uh . . . it's not that kind of a story.

ED: Material for you, yeah.

ME: It's just . . . yeah . . . I'll use it or I won't, whatever it is. Some of the things are supposed to be just . . . uh . . . a serious question as though I were really *interviewing* you about *art* or something like that.

ED: Right.

ME: So . . . and if it . . . Tell you what, if the answer goes on and there seems to be *enough*, I'll stop you.

ED: Good.

ME: Even when you're not through.

ED: Good. You know me, especially after a couple of drinks.

ME: Uh . . . because sometimes it's just . . . I just want . . . uh . . . like a little answer.

ED: Right.

ME: . . . or something like that. So we'll just begin. Well, these are kind of mixed up but I can straighten them out later. Um . . . O.K. Now what's the thing about yourself that you like the least? Have you ever thought of that?

ED: Of course I have.

ME: Well, I never heard about it.

ED: All right.

ME: Don't get mad. What *is* the thing about yourself you like least?

ED: Well, all right . . . Uh . . . It's my fearfulness, though that probably will surprise some people, and maybe making films is a way of coping with things in an indirect way and yet . . . well, film making's scary, too. Actually the frightful thing about it is that you *have* to be aggressive and you *have* to be someone who takes a masculine role and . . . well, I'm fearful of it because you've got to perform, which I suppose it's the old proving yourself thing and you constantly have to do it over and over and that's a terrible drag. Film making is a little bit like sex in those terms. . . . Oh, of course it can also be just pure joy . . . just an easy thing, too.

ME: Sex is a fearful thing, too?

ED: Oh, yeah, in those terms.

ME: Well, is it even fearful with someone that you know, like me? I guess it is.

ED: Well, yeah, we've had enough conflicts in those terms.

ME: Do you feel fearful a lot? . . . All the time?

ED: I'm not conscious of it like that, but I . . . I, at one time, was thinking that the major governing factor almost . . . this is probably stupid psychology . . . was fear. People behave as they do because they're afraid to act otherwise.

ME: Well, I think you're right, in a sense, because, just having read a little of that Grotowski book, you get the sense that what he's doing is undoing . . . uh . . . the masks . . .

ED: Well, basically, I think that a lot of the behavior patterns we have are designed to protect us and . . . but when I say that what I, in a way, fear most is my own fearfulness, that's probably not true, except it's the one thing that I feel if I could just not be afraid in lots of ways, I could do *everything*.

ME: Maybe people think they'd dance and sing and make speeches if they weren't afraid but maybe they'd really just feel perfectly comfortable to sit quietly in a corner . . .

ED: . . . and you face your fears frequently. In other words, when I make a movie, the reason I have a hard time is that it's so damn difficult to organize things and make sure that I'm not making mistakes. Lots of people think of me as very calm . . . um, externally . . . and very easygoing. Actually when I'm shooting there's a tremendous amount of anxiety because even though I'm also regarded as someone who is very competent with equipment and so forth, I constantly have a feeling as though I don't know what the hell's happening behind this piece of machinery and . . . and I hope that it's going to come out right. So, obviously, the way we overcome fear usually is by going through and doing things we fear most.

ME: Well, you're probably doing it for a lot of reasons . . . maybe a lot of other reasons, too. Well, why are you doing it?

ED: Doing what?

ME: Making movies?

ED: Well, now, you see, the thing is . . . it gets down to one of these . . . uh . . . another aspect of . . . but I think the artist really . . . they like to play God. It's the opposite of being fearful. You are running things. You have control. It's the other side of the coin. I suppose it's all out of the same mix.

ME: Well, it's funny, though, like with *Branches* you got this big mishmash of material . . . that you'd think a person would be panic-stricken to have because it was so out of control in a certain way, but maybe it never seemed that way to you.

ED: Well, now, that's another thing about the way I make a movie. I like to *not* have control. . . .

ME: You like to find the control.

ED: Yeah, and I like to have the excitement of going out into uncharted territory and seeing if I can get through it and it's fearful and it's exhilarating at the same time.

ME: It must be very satisfying, like with *Branches*, where you didn't know what was going to happen . . .

ED: Right.

ME: . . . to feel that you came out with something formed.

ED: But I don't mind entering a film project feeling that it can go bust. I like the idea of . . . and I've insisted on it in my own personal work . . . of *not* having it completely locked down in advance . . . have it be open-ended enough so that I really don't know what the final form is going to be and I can just explore the adventure of making it.

ME: That's how I'm doing this story. . . . Well, O.K. I'll cut a lot of this out but this ought to be enough.

So . . .

Thank you, Ed.

Thank you for sex.

And thanks again for a lot of little things you do and sitting talking together over a hamburger and coffee.

And thank you for a male body and a penis, a male voice, a nice male hand, and male shirts, male underwear, socks, pants and T-shirts, also beards, hairy legs, things like that.

Thanks a lot.

"Hey, there, eager poets of all ages . . ."

I would like to thank them, too. I would like to thank the poets. I would especially like to thank poets such as Ron Padgett and Tom Disch and Frank O'Hara and George Quasha and Jerome Rothenberg, but most of all Ed, without whom this could not have been written.

Yes, Virginia

I was the first woman to stay awake for 206 consecutive hours in a telephone booth.

I was the first woman to sink in quicksand up to my forehead and still survive.

I was the first woman to have my face carved out of the living rock a thousand feet high.

I was the first woman to see and to assess in twenty-five words or less the Abominable Snowman from thousands of feet above sea level.

I was the first woman to copulate with a porpoise named Harry under thirty feet of water.

I was the first woman to write twenty-nine poems on love with two radios and a TV set turned on in the same room.

After an unproductive summer, I found myself at loose ends in a medium-sized midwestern town. I was (understandably) shipwrecked on an uninhabited island off the coast of California and I had taken a one-room apartment in the middle of an emotional desert over a bookstore owned by a white, middle-class and aging bachelor.

I had experienced a crisis of collective guilt.

I had thought about the universe.

I was tired.

"Give me," I said, "informal interpersonal relationships, a rent-controlled apartment, and one little avant-garde love affair."

"Right now," I said, "all I might ask is to join a company of wandering street performers." I would play both heroes and heroines. I would sing songs and do the most modern of dances rather like Yvonne Rainer's in style. I would, I hoped, find myself surrounded by active, simple people, psychologically oriented toward the good of humanity in the best sense of the words.

(But this was not to be. At least not at this moment.)

(I just wonder sometimes why life is like that.)

Meanwhile I wandered the streets at dangerous hours of the night while thousands of Communist Chinese were staging a protest demonstration in front of the Soviet embassy and four American airmen were being detained in Cambodia.

Three flights up and turn left twice above the bookstore and I was already lost in the mist and hearing the beginnings of a number of disparate conversations. I met several creatures resembling human beings in every respect but one. (I had found my way ashore on a rubber life raft. I had brought enough Tampax to last six months. I hoped to find some sort of man Friday in a few weeks. I had seen footprints in the sand.) This would be an unusual opportunity to experience, at first hand, social customs with which I was totally unfamiliar.

I prepared for departure bright and early the next morning, hoping to take a trip into the outlying districts. I was thinking that these creatures might have an entirely different way of love-making. They reminded me of walruses or manatees. Sex seemed their natural element. They organized around it, read it, talked it, liberated it, rehearsed it, delayed it, policed it, entertained with it. They had thirty-three different words for fuck with all different shades of vulgarity, each one denoting a slightly different position. (They had no word for perversion.)

Under circumstances like this I think of myself as a sea slug, sea cucumber, caterpillar or soft, white-underbellied thing, psychic energy concentrated in the mucous-membranous areas. What would Antonin Artaud have thought had he seen me from some high insane asylum window, my typewriter on my back, a mechanical means of birth control in my pocket, a guttural (Artaudish) shout on my lips?

"An honest expression of the life force," he said.

I laughed and changed the subject.

(Life is like that.)

"What I'm really waiting for," I said, "is much more than love."

I wanted a monument to myself in granite. I wanted my face in seven different colors. I wanted I LOVE YOU in giant red letters on top of the Museum of Modern Art. I wanted a new bridge across the Hudson in my name. I wanted a three-volume history of the Greeks dedicated to my memory. I wanted a filmed version of my life in Ektachrome commercial. I wanted the Mercedes-Benz no longer to be for Mercedes.

But I have small breasts.

I have been to the edge of the desert, to the brink of disaster. I have looked into the abyss. I have seen Medusa and told about it afterward. I have looked back and not been changed into a pillar of salt. I have married my father/mother and not put out my eyes. I have had my mother's love withheld from me, my psychological needs not met. I have spoken the secret name of God.

And I did enter the outlying districts and suffered strange vicissitudes. These were not the cultural centers, these islands full of back roads, distant horizons and vast, featureless plains, still some things went on here, and just living over a bookstore was a romantic thing for me. I had had three or four children and this was a change. I had come a long way since then if one measures in time passed and things forgotten. Measured in microseconds, my life was already equal to the age of life on earth. I was already as old as some of the (younger) stones, and if the area I've covered in any given year was reduced to the size of football fields and laid end to end, I imagine it might cover Manhattan Island twice at least, or reach to Boston.

But I must have gone to sleep (or passed out) without meaning to, because when I woke up I was on the opposite shore and of quite another opinion and had already made friends with one of them in spite of myself, taming him with nuts and raisins and letting him sleep on my couch on rainy afternoons. We had made love four or five times his way, and I'm glad we did. I established the kind of contact and gained a kind of knowledge that couldn't be had any other way. I served as an outlet for his exotic longings, he as my informant. As soon as I learned their dialect, I asked him how many moons could be in their sky at the same time at any given moment.

Many of the things they believe in are true.

We've all been fooled at one time or another by complicated forms of expression, by blaming the system or by negative results. We've all taken rowboats out on a sunny day and come home in the rain. Little things like that. We've all been betrayed by our own kindnesses or our satisfactions. I, myself, have hardly ever been the exception to any rule and so I may have misunderstood my informant as thoroughly as anybody might. Psychologists agree, nine out of ten people come to faulty conclusions. Wearing my white pith helmet, I've gone through life this way, halfway to my knees, half on tiptoe, so it's no coincidence that I wanted to bring him back home with me, but that would have been, of course, unkind. (Our air is so much denser.) If I was to have any feeling for this little fellow creature, I must leave him in his own natural habitat to grow and develop as he himself might see fit. Besides, the governor asked me not to, saying: "How would he find happiness, or better still, real joy so far from his home islands?" Abraham Maslow might have noticed me at dawn there, weeping as I left, and he might have had many comments to make about self-actualizing people, and Marcuse might have said that I had done the right thing in the Freudian way.

So, in my short skirts, flat-heeled shoes and sunglasses, with a bemused expression on my wind-burned face, I had said good-bye to him in a perfectly natural way, squinting at their huge red sun one last time before embarking. (I had eaten six pomegranate seeds and answered each of their questions twelve different ways. I had slept on palm fronds.) (I planned to mail him a package every other week and send a telegram confessing my love, but all of that much later. . . .)

Theirs were strange ways, poetry as prevalent as prose, a musician in every home, aphrodisiacs directly from the jar. They have longer days off than we do, livelier looks in their eyes, blonder hair, and mine was thoroughly one of them.

I used to hold him on my lap.

But I was well aware that I would have to leave him soon and I wanted to foster all his drives outward toward his own kind and away from me. This was done the reverse of the taming procedures, again using nuts and raisins and an occasional reinforcing electric shock. I dumped him off both my lap and my couch though we did continue to have sex together, but *my* way. (I sometimes wonder, is Freud relevant to the lower beings? I have often felt an affinity to planarian worms, especially when they can't make up their minds.)

A few days after returning I believe I may have met my husband in the back row of the balcony. I thought it was him. I said, "Excuse me," and stepped on his toe. It's hard to say if I did it on purpose or not. It was dark and I was late. I thought I felt his hand touch my breast or the inner part of my thigh. I wanted to ask him if we had ever had any children together and if we'd ever thought about them but I held myself back. "I'm sorry I stepped on your toe, Earth man," I said (actually I really was).

Well, that was fun on a theoretical level and even the play was good but I wouldn't want to repeat it. He is an assistant professor in a department of pure science. "Industrial research laboratories are getting all the grants," he said. Once I asked him, "Let me see you dressed as a woman," but he was a man of principles.

Tell me, M. Levi-Strauss, have I by chance contaminated the natives with any false ideas or forms of government that might be unacceptable to any later explorers? Did I open the windows of their minds too soon for this stage of their evolution? Did I sow seeds that would destroy their art forms before they reached their highest stages of fruition? Did I even bring in some sort of smallpox germ on my blankets? Did they really all die? Empty apartments? All the artifacts intact? (The only sherds are in the garbage cans?) The governor long since dead? The aging homosexual? Also my little friend and lover? Creature of the little, tickly, stringlike penis? My apartment over the bookstore, for all that, still intact?

I have sought to gain time. Kept out of sight for three months. I have written letters to the editors. I've canceled my subscription to the *Realist*. I've even thought of returning to my husband, adopting a child or getting married again to an airlines pilot or a train conductor. But what does it matter?

"I don't mind being spit at or pissed on," I said. "I make a lot of little slips myself."

I may have one more thing to tell them before the trap door is opened or the sergeant of the firing squad says, "Fire." In fact I'm sure of it. "Wait," I'll say.

The Childhood of the
Human Hero*

A little bit of you in him and a little bit of me and a little bit of him in you and I see a bit of my youngest brother. He's coming in, going out, coming in, going out, and it's another world outside which might be inner space which is outer space to him. "Captain, your ship is approaching a doomed planet at twice the speed of light."

He wants to order a pair of handcuffs at $2.95.
A book on ventriloquism at ninety-eight cents.
He wants a realistic plastic plucked chicken, $5.99.
A pair of sunglasses with one-way-mirror lenses.
A "patented 3D hypno-coin" that comes free with twenty-five lessons in hypnotism.
And one hundred stick-on stamps of the scariest movie monster.

Mild-mannered boy wonder looks like any other average boy, but there's a trick to it. There's more than meets the eye and good deeds are being done every day in spite of appearances.
He has a secret identity.

* The title is quoted from Joseph Campbell.

Going into orbit around one hot world too many, he breaks pencils with a flick of the fingers of one hand and doesn't know he's doing it. He straightens paper clips trying to remember that France has a population of 51,400,000; that the major cities are: Paris, Lille, Bordeaux, Marseilles; highest point, Mont Blanc, 15,781 feet; principal language, French.

He's the one with the new boots, just the kind he's always wanted; wide belt, black turtleneck sweater. Next year his hair will be even longer because that's the only way you can tell the kids in the Common Concern Club from the Young Americans for Freedom.

When he grows a mustache (this much later) it'll be the long yellow/brown kind that curls up at the ends and he'll be smiling.

Say, did you know there's a new method that can give you powerful muscles you'll be proud to show your friends in just ten minutes a day? "Carry your great strength with prudence and humility," I say, but you've broken another ballpoint pen writing the answer to the problem of farmer Brown who plows half an acre in twenty minutes and farmer Jones who has plowed thirty-two acres in seventy-six hours.

He's coming in, going out, coming in, going out. It's another world entirely outside and that waltz is really the original motion picture sound track from *2001*.

I know you. I was almost a boy once myself, mother though I have become, and I know it might as well be . . . maybe ought to be Chichén Itzá instead of Betelgeuse or someplace with a lot of moons. You'll lose all that, you know, Captain, next year or the year after, but there will be greater losses, and that sonic blast was just a stalling tactic to keep you busy while they roll out this monstrous world. You have yet to face the bureaucratic creatures that crawl through rocks and can hold you helplessly imprisoned in megaliths even though you may be in telepathic contact with the big-brained friends of this universe. There are things you'd never suspect out here in reality land and your night terrors are nothing compared to them. You won't recognize him. I mean that man with the yellow/brown mustache coming in for a landing on some different planet farther in the future than you ever thought possible. He's of the next century, you know, and will be at his peak by 2001. Did you realize that yesterday when you asked me, "What does 'existential' mean?" and I couldn't answer so you knew? "Forget it," you said and I can't forget it, because without your existential superself you will certainly perish in wars of the future out among the satellites, overcome by cosmic thought patterns too convoluted for the human brain to contemplate, or, if not that, torn apart by humanoids in the death throes of their own identity crises, or exploded by technological advances available not only to the future, but known already to the present, and, if not one or more of the above, inevitably coarsened by Earthlings of your own kind. I can't save you, because even though thunder sends the cats under the bed and still brings you into my room, where there can be no ghosts, no tigers, and monsters still shrivel up and die when I turn on the lights, my powers are fading. But I'm not, repeat, not waiting for you to grow up, because that's another thing entirely.

"What's the size of a shark's brain?"
"What's the capital of Colorado?"
"What's the longest book ever written?"
"What's green and warty and lives at the bottom of the sea?"

For Mother, on Mother's day, draw spaceships.

Learn it, dummy. 8 × 7, 8 × 8. "You're making me hate arithmetic," he says. Odd numbers, even numbers, two by two down school's light-green halls and he's been at it seven years. Even when there's a death, you know, we all go on more or less as though nothing had happened. Go back to those same old circumferences of circles, parallel lines down the middle of, and follow instructions. I'm telling you, you can do as you wish, see the dead laid out on display the old-fashioned way with a hundred and fifty-dollar blanket of roses just as Grandma wanted it, or not. It's up to you. But don't come to me after five o'clock because there's no changing your mind. There's a death deadline, but it's not what you think, falling down and losing your memory, getting up and falling down again, the sudden zap, zap, zap of ray guns. You've lost some of your best men, but you're miraculously safe. Captain, you're always so miraculously safe except in the dark.

Slide inner front sprocket wheel (#17) over sprocket shaft, then place wheel retainer (#13) over end of shaft. Apply a drop of cement to end of shaft adhering retainer to shaft. Then cement outer front sprocket wheel (#18) to inner sprocket wheel by applying cement at notch on outer wheel.
"Look, Ma. Look, Ma."
(Don't bother me now.)
"Look, Ma, drop these seemingly innocent pellets into a glass of water and magically a worm will appear."

By 2001 I'll be dead.
No more "Look, Ma."

Inferno, mad inventor of instruments of torture and destruction, all your tricks are useless. They can't make him tell where his mother is hidden.

For those who dare! SURPRISE PACKAGE. Only fifty cents. Are you willing to take a chance on a secret? Listen then: the mother has both breasts and penis sometimes. She *has* to. There's no other solution to some of those knotty little problems of sexual identification; face them every day and see who wears the blue jeans. (Everybody does.) We won't tell you what *you* get, but because you're willing to gamble we'll give you much more than your money's worth. Satisfaction guaranteed. Are you willing to face the *real* green slime? Well, let's get this straightened out once and for all. Maybe the penis is just a realistic skin-colored spooky hand with red fingernails and big knuckles (ninety-eight cents). Imagine it poking out of your car door at sixty miles an hour, or out of a suitcase on the train. Imagine it on the piano keys, on the window ledge, peeking out of a grocery bag, opening a door. Comes with special adhesive. Sticks anywhere. Can be reused over and over and over and over.

What's green and squashed and lies in the gutter? That's a girl scout run over by a truck.

There are still some wishes left and crazy laughter and a secret handshake. But after a while you face life at your own risk.

When, in the course of human events, evidence comes to light of evil forces overpowering the good, give that boy three impossible tasks to do to restore the world to its proper place among the respectable planets. Steadfast and true. Honorable unto the death, of course. Helper of the helpless. Kind to animals. Honesty his best policy. Oh, incorruptible boy, I see the faint new moon float past your head one midafternoon. The clouds hardly moving and you blasting off into one of those lazy Sundays with an Estes rocket. "Gentlemen, we're limping back to Aldebaran. We've slipped out of space warp and into real time. We're lost in an out-of-the-way section of deep space and who knows what evil lurks among the stars? . . ."

Back here we're waiting for all systems to be go, for all men to be safe and accounted for and in real time and serving a different purpose. It's another world going on outside and might be airless. Suit up, men, preferably in silver, then gasping (gasp, gasp), falling down. "Look, Ma, honorable unto the death."

What's green and squashed and lies in the gutter? Well, there's a war on and it's this world now and it could be you with your new yellow/brown mustache.

But that boy doesn't belong on this planet at all. Someday his real father and mother will come down to claim him and take him back where he belongs. He'll be homesick for his former Earth family for a while, but after a week or so it'll be all right. The new life will be hard, but rewarding. He will accompany his new father in a ship, preferably all in silver, and go from planet to planet doing one good deed every day, 365 good deeds every Earth year.

That last blast-off almost poked a hole right through the ceiling. "I wouldn't do that in here again if I. . . ."
Beaming down while the cosmic energy still burns within him, shouts, "Wait, I know just what you're going to say and I don't want to hear it."
(But maybe it's just one of those imitation bullet holes at nine for fifty cents.)

Husband, ours is indeed an admirable boy, but don't expose his secret identity: "seven toes to each foot and to either hand as many fingers; his eyes, bright with seven pupils. On each cheek he has four moles, a blue, a red, a green, a purple. Between one ear and the other, long yellow tresses that are as yellow as the wax of bees . . ."*

*From the Book of Leinster, translated by Eleanor Hull, quoted by Joseph Campbell in *The Hero with a Thousand Faces.*

Animal

The first day of the animal the sun came up yellow over fog. A woman from the Century Arms apartments walked her three dogs early but hurried back within ten minutes. Her breath was visible. Later on, a man, carrying a cane and wearing a tan overcoat, paused at the corner of the small park where the woman had walked the dogs and buttoned up his collar. The sun of the first day of the animal had, by now, turned orange and the man's breath was not visible. The animal, as might be expected on his first morning, slept late. At eleven he was given a bowl of shredded wheat, a glass of milk and two slices of buttered toast but he refused to eat any of it. This was expected, too. He did, however, drink sixteen ounces of water from a pail left in the corner for him and this was considered a very good sign.

He was found, of course, in the deepest part of the forest.

The second day of the animal all the windows frosted over. People woke up early and even the night watchmen went home whistling. Something in the air. The barometer was rising. The man of the tan overcoat took ten deep breaths, blowing out alternately from the right and left nostril. The woman who loves dogs enjoyed the cold on this, the second morning. She has never been married and she has a history of dating unsuitable men in spite of the dignity and self-assurance of her posture.

The animal still does not eat. He has watched out the window for a long time. What is he dreaming? his keepers wonder, that confinement is a question of degree? measured less by bars than by the perspectives behind them? by the vistas from the windows of his third-floor room in the office building of the keepers and hunters, so the question may not be, after all: Are the doors locked? but Where would they lead to once they are opened, if such a time might ever come? And are the answers, whatever they may be, all the freedoms he can hope for?

It was said, on the second day, that he did not look too unhappy. At lunchtime a keeper of a particular sensitivity brought him both a grilled cheese sandwich and a hamburger so that it might be seen what his preferences were, but still he ate nothing.

Some intelligence seems to shine in his eyes. The keepers all feel he may be conscious of some meaning in their words, no doubt interpreting them in his own way. The keepers say he may dimly understand the significance of his position in their midst. Perhaps he wishes for more elements from which to draw conclusions. One keeper feels that if he had a drum and a flute he might make some kind of music and these are supplied but he only taps his fingers on his chin.

There's much to do: wash him, cut his nails, clip his mane. (All those curls and, underneath, his head is found to be the same size as everyone's.)

There are no marks of the capture on the animal except where the ropes had rubbed into his wrists and ankles. It was said he had suffered no more than a nosebleed at the time and yet he had killed two of the hunters with his bare hands. They had dropped him as they entered the city early that morning. He was tied, hands and feet, to a pole and supported by four of them and they had come into the city singing rounds and swinging him jauntily. This was after the last bus had gone back to the center and after the last bus driver had gone to bed and not a taxi in sight. They had stumbled as they came down the embankment and he hit the sidewalk with the back of his head and grunted. His nose began to bleed again; however, many of the hunters had had worse than that from him so not one of them thought to apologize.

On the third day the animal ate—scrambled eggs and bacon, toast, orange juice—and it was considered that the most important hurdles were over and, since the weather continued fair, it was felt by most of them that no one would object if the animal was allowed some fresh air in some small nearby park, provided some pants could be put on him and kept on. Still, it was argued by a minority that this was not necessary for an animal. Others said that it wasn't at all a philosophical question as to when and when not animals might need to wear trousers or even what might constitute animalness, but more a question of simple physiology and that anyone with eyes could answer it and, what's more, would answer it undoubtedly in favor of pants.

Since the keepers all dress alike in gray coveralls, it was decided that one of these would be the simplest to keep on him and, with a small combination lock at the top of the zipper, there could be no danger that the animal might remove them himself at some inappropriate time.

The woman walks her dogs four times a day. She is tall and always wears black or white with a red hat. Father figures tempt her, hunters and keepers, men she can count on to give her advice and encouragement though one wouldn't suspect this from her assured attitudes.

The animal is graying at the temples. His eyebrows have grown bushy. There are hairs in his ears. Perhaps his hard life in the deepest part of the forest has aged him. Actually the man in the tan coat appears to be the same age and might make a proper husband even though he hasn't yet been married and, at his time of life, one would suspect strange vices. Yet he could afford a wife and he has kept himself remarkably fit. He doesn't smoke. Unfortunately he never passes the Century Arms at quite the right times for any chance meetings to occur and neither do the animal and the woman meet, this third day, but if he has an odor, subtle and savage, that is certainly what makes her take off her white scarf and open the top button of her coat. What if she is conscious of some secret origins? (Perhaps all the townspeople are.) Then she may feel some organic kinship at this smell and from it she might draw conclusions about her past and maybe even about her future. Now the dogs slink with their tails between their legs. They are black retrievers though she can have no use for their inborn talents at the Century Arms. The only water they ever see is in their bowls or rain but the weather continues fair. It grows warmer. It is thought that the animal might be permanently installed in the small park, where he would see the sun and yet be out of the public's way to some extent. It is thought an imitation cave with a heater and a cot might do well enough and a private bathroom with shower stall. Some keepers wonder if even a heavy wire mesh will be strong enough to hold him. It must cross the top of the cage for he is nimble enough to climb almost anything with a toehold. There happens to be a suitable spot there already which once housed squirrels, foxes, a raccoon and an owl. It only needs enlarging and refurnishing.

Chance encounters sometimes lead to warm friendships and at their first meeting she offers the animal a cigarette which he accepts graciously with a little nod of thanks. Unfortunately, under these circumstances, she would have to play rather the dominating role in the relationship and yet appearances are so important that his expression alone may lead her to believe in his abilities as adviser and encourager. The mesh makes things simpler in many ways. She might bring him little presents of coffee in containers to go, or ice cream or something she has baked herself, and she will never need to wonder why he hasn't brought anything to her. She can put herself in a mother role and act out a part she would prefer he played, perhaps thinking he will learn from her, yearning to tuck blankets round his chin, to rub his back, always speaking softly.

Others come and watch him as they watch the goldfish in the

pond or how far the crocus has come up. Someone has somehow taken pictures of him naked and sold them surreptitiously. The man in the tan overcoat bought a set of five but he doesn't meet the woman that day in front of the animal's cage as the creature chins himself on a branch of his ginkgo tree. If he were here, she might pay some attention to the man in the tan coat, more than she ordinarily would. Everything has become physical and even under their overcoats they would have felt themselves to be there in the flesh.

Neither of them has yet received the invitation to the party that will celebrate the installation of the animal in the park. There has been a delay in hopes that warmer weather will come in the next week or two. The hunters and keepers will be there as well as most of the people in the nearby apartments such as the Century Arms. It is felt that perhaps the animal will pick up some valuable hints on the nature of civilized behavior from this event, though, of course, he can't be blamed for the two killings that occurred at his capture. Some of the townspeople have wondered what would have happened at that time had he been captured by other townspeople than hunters, had, for instance, the behaviorists come upon him first, or the Freudians, or more especially the Jungians. Some of the keepers themselves, and many have become quite fond of him, argue that there would have been no deaths, yet others say he has turned on them in anger more than once, though they managed to get out of his way in time, but they can't say for sure if these were only threatening gestures.

Yet suddenly, before the invitations can be sent, the animal escapes. No one can understand quite how. At night there's the policeman to check now and then. The lights are kept burning all around the park and yet he's gone. There are reports of four rapes that night, and goodness knows, the townspeople say, how many unreported. One can't be sure who committed them. (There has already been much thought about his possible animal wife or wives, his animal children, perhaps whole colonies of animals living in shelters under the roots of fallen trees, nested in coarse skins and covered with lice. Perhaps they run in packs.) In any case, it may well be that the women of the townspeople seem extraordinarily desirable to him or perhaps it's just his superb physical shape or his animal nature and maybe he isn't responsible for the rapes at all.

Once the woman had come in late afternoon and whispered "Apartment 5A" as though by some miracle he could come to her open window five floors up. Many of the townspeople have exaggerated ideas of the animal's abilities, but still, he has escaped miraculously, no one can tell how. Perhaps as he shaved himself in the mornings, his thoughts had turned to the functioning of doors and locks and maybe the woman had left him a bobby pin or dropped one by the wire mesh where he could reach it. Perhaps the key to her apartment, by some strange coincidence, also fit the door of his cage.

And certainly, these moonlight nights, the woman would have liked to reinvent love on a higher plane, liked to consider it from many angles and choose those most likely to satisfy in the longest run of all. And suppose there are to be thoughts also on the new man or a new mankind? a new movement of which the animal might be the leader and she might play the role of sister to the animal, a position without emotional dangers, in which she can permit herself a certain degree of closeness while waiting for some ritual sacrifices to take place. And she wants love tests also for herself to pass, and a period of fasting, a building up of muscles and mental capacities, some way to prepare herself while she waits for his token, a severed finger, ear or toe. Who knows what rites he practices? These days the ceremonials among the townspeople are dying out. Who remembers what the wedding ring really stands for?

She must have remembered to be happy in spite of a lack of participation in that first night of the escape, and he must have remembered to be careful not to let his beard grow.

He was found ten days later eating a hamburger and French fries in a diner in a distant city, wearing an astrakhan hat, sunglasses and smoking Marlboros. He did not resist recapture and was taken by taxi to the airport with no incidents. Positive identification wasn't difficult even though he had changed his name and adopted many new mannerisms.

A double lock is put upon his door and a guard to warn the townspeople not to come too near. It is felt new hobbies will have to be found to occupy his time. Someone has contributed an old upright piano. Others have brought last month's magazines, paint sets, colored pencils, a banjo. There is a general understanding among the townspeople that there comes a time in everyone's life when new decisions must be made, new directions taken, new resolutions formulated. The townspeople recognize this phase as it becomes manifest in the actions and attitudes of the animal. After all, he is, they estimate, at about that age when such a change is due, and he must understand, in some vague way of his own, that in spite of his marvelous physical condition, he has passed the peak of his powers, so they are watching the new self-awarenesses bloom in him along with new generosities and new dissatisfactions. Surely he is asking not only what is the purpose of life, but more specifically, what will he make the purpose of his own life. Now he takes up new pleasures and discards old ones. He revolves slowly to music by the townspeople's best-loved long-dead composers. He dances with his eyes shut. He taps on the mesh. He seems to understand or at least to react to counterpoint and fugue. He receives a daily newspaper and a good deal of mail addressed to occupant. He writes: Once I crouched, flea-bitten, eating raw roots. Once I never heard of shirt tails, socks and tie tacks. I slept on ferns.

By now it is the fifty-first day of the animal.

He is writing poems on shredded-wheat cardboards and old envelopes, but this time of year the younger townspeople roller skate in the park. The sound of their wheels on the sidewalks bothers the animal as he sits thinking what to write down next or when he is studying a book on style. He has a list of nouns expressing movement and a note to remind himself to put a short sentence next to a long one. Lately he has studied the role of mystery in fiction of every form, but now, probably because of some special feeling for the lady with the dogs and knowing her address from before, he writes: Dear Madam: I must apologize for the night of April second, 1965. . . . She won't be sure what he is apologizing for even though it was not a fulfilled night for her as it may have been for the animal.

He has already attended two cocktail parties in his honor and one literary tea and he has returned to his cage without complaint. The extra guard may soon be removed. Someone has given him a tan corduroy jacket with leather patches on the elbows. Many townspeople have found him extraordinarily attractive, especially in a cocktail party setting. The combination of a rugged, even dangerous-looking face, white teeth, a well-cut jacket, a delicate touch upon a martini glass and a bit of primeval shyness is irresistible and none of the male townspeople have blamed the female townspeople for their susceptibility. One woman has sent him three bottles of champagne, another a suede vest and an imported shoehorn. One has knit him a sweater, which he will certainly put to good use since the heating in his cave is not particularly good and the imitation-stone door has never closed well. He would have liked an electric blanket, which might not have been any more expensive than the champagne, but he certainly must know that he cannot choose in his position.

One woman has asked if he might be let out in her custody. She has, no doubt, realized the distractions of the park with its roller skating and its gaping visitors, with even the guard wanting to join into some sort of communication with the animal. She has felt this isn't in the best interests of his art.

She would like to install him in a section of her summer house where he might have a suite of rooms over the garage. She hopes he will be of use as a fourth for bridge and secretly she imagines that the animal will not be aware of her age as she is interested in a certain aspect of his animal nature. The morals of a case like this may be questioned, but the answer is certainly not clear-cut.

But this would be just for the Easter vacation and perhaps for next summer. Of course, she realizes that the townspeople need this attraction for their park and that the animal belongs to all the people and not just to her but she feels he needs a change if only for the sake of his art. Where will his new ideas come from? she asks, and wouldn't a wild creature do better in the suburbs than in the center of town? at least for a while? People must have sympathy and understanding for all the wild creatures and if she can't have this one she might consider taking a gibbon instead, or a young fox.

She has already gone to the jewelers to have a silver chain made with which to lead him to breakfast, lunch and dinner.

But he has written: Dear Madam: I would like to accept your kind offer of the use of your house in the country, but I'm afraid I have other plans over Easter. However, I may be available for the summer, especially after August first. Perhaps you will consider some alternatives since, as you are well aware, all of us wild creatures would enjoy a week outside the town. I would suggest you contact the keepers as to which animals will be the most suitable. Very truly yours, the animal.

The young male townspeople imitate the animal. They stand at the street corners with their heads at a noble angle, their cigarettes between thumb and forefinger. They all have political opinions now and they fondle stray cats.

The woman still walks her dogs four times a day as usual. She has bought three red leashes for them.

There is much conjecture as to whether the animal is actually capable of experiencing real love in spite of the complications of his political beliefs and the nuances of his art. One never knows how imitative such things may be. But it does look as though the animal considers the three dogs exceptionally graceful. It looks as though he is interested in becoming friendly with the dogs, but he has recently given up smoking and there is no longer any excuse for her offering him cigarettes. Perhaps cough drops if he coughs a bit and she notices, but she doesn't.

There are changes afoot. Professors have come to study his reflexes and they have found that they are in no way different from those of the townspeople. This hasn't surprised anyone since they have all, long ago, recognized their animal origins. Yet there is a general sense of foreboding. There has been a reorganization in the department of parks. Younger townspeople are coming in to replace older men. There will certainly be new theories on the influences of such a creature as the animal living in plain view of everyone. Many studies are already under way as to whether there has been more or less crime since his capture. Attitudes of the teen-age townspeople are being questioned by teams of graduate students and the animal's writings are being studied by experts in animal behavior. The animal himself has expressed the view that he would like to be considered as an individual as well as an animal. Soon there will be a symposium. Everyone has a theory or two. The lady with the three dogs will be there as a representative of the citizens' council of residents of the park area. It is said that the animal himself will preside as chairman, though he will have no real say in the proceedings. No doubt it will be broadcast.

The animal has not yet expressed any opinion of his own. Most likely he is waiting for the results of the various studies to be published. The townspeople are eagerly waiting for him to speak out, for they are sure, as with all his writings, that what he says will not be ordinary.

The woman with the dogs feels her responsibilities deeply and is even more inclined to wear black than ever, but she still allows herself red leashes. She doesn't think it proper for her to discuss anything with the animal at the present time.

On sunny Sundays the park is full of dogs including the three with the red leashes. Townspeople who own dogs can always find something to talk about with each other. It's too bad the animal doesn't own a dog. There is so much he could have joined into. Later the townspeople will remember this and think: If only we had given him a dog since he had to live in the park, anyway. But of course it's too late now.

He has evidently come to a decision and walked away into the deepest part of the forest without writing a single word on the question of his good or bad influences. He has left all the townspeople with an empty feeling inside. Their park seems deserted.

The woman walks with her head up. There are rumors about her but nothing anyone can prove. Her dogs act as though they own the park. Not a single tree is sacred to them. Many townspeople wonder, were they really that way before? What if she has shown the animal some secret results from some secret studies? Had she some information not yet released to the general public? Or is it that she has finally grown bold enough to realize her love and confess it? and was he, after all, capable of some sort of loving response of the same nature as the townspeople's responses? But how will they ever know now all that their animal might have been capable of? And they will always be wondering why he went just at this particular time, before the symposium had even begun. They will think how great was his need to return to the land of his origin. They will say he pined for his animal family, his possible animal wives and children, or they will say that he searches for his youth in the places where he once was young or that it is for the townspeople's sake, because of his influence, perhaps sinister and yet so subtle only he was aware of it, that he has hidden himself there, alone and lonely, writing his poems out on birch bark and whistling themes from the music of their long-dead composers, able to avoid capture this time because of his greater knowledge of the townspeople's methods.

Oh, come back to us, they sometimes call out silently toward the forest, come and write us your animal opinions. Sit in our park. Adorn our cocktail parties. Crime wave or no, you were really good for us in the long run, and even if that may not be true, why, you belonged to us and no other town had one like you.

But there's nothing for them to do but to await the sons and daughters of the animal, those conceived on the nights of freedom, if it really was the animal who was responsible for (and capable of) that rash of rapes. Will the children of the animal, they wonder, follow him back to the deepest part of the forest by instinct, off in search of their father as soon as they are old enough? And what of the youngest? the one that some of the townspeople believe must have been conceived the night he left: will he or she stay as a gift to the townspeople from the animal, decorating first their schools, their birthday parties, baseball games, even roller skating in the very park where her father spent so much of his time, later the college, the dances, contributing to the courses in logic and philology, majoring in history or French and then marrying one of the townspeople and conceiving sons and daughters of her own?

Surely, the townspeople think, surely the blood of the animal is with us still and will, in some future time, be a part of us all.

Sex and / or Mr. Morrison

I can set my clock by Mr. Morrison's step upon the stairs, not that he is that accurate, but accurate enough for me. Eight-thirty, thereabouts. (My clock runs fast, anyway.) Each day he comes clumping down and I set it back ten minutes, or eight minutes or seven. I suppose I could just as well do it without him but it seems a shame to waste all that heavy treading and those puffs and sighs of expanding energy on only getting downstairs, so I have timed my life to this morning beat. Funereal tempo, one might well call it, but it is funereal only because Mr. Morrison is fat and therefore slow. Actually he's a very nice man as men go. He always smiles.

I wait downstairs, sometimes looking up and sometimes holding my alarm clock. I smile a smile I hope is not as wistful as his. Mr. Morrison's moon face has something of the *Mona Lisa* to it. Certainly he must have secrets.

"I'm setting my clock by you, Mr. M."

"Heh, heh . . . my, my," grunt, breath. "Well," heave the stomach to the right, "I hope . . ."

"Oh, you're on time enough for *me.*"

"Heh, heh. Oh. Oh, yes." The weight of the world is surely upon him or perhaps he's crushed and flattened by a hundred miles of air. How many pounds per square inch weighing him down? He hasn't the inner energy to push back. All his muscles spread like jelly under his skin.

"No time to talk," he says. (He never has time.) Off he goes. I like him and his clipped little Boston accent, but I know he's too proud ever to be friendly. Proud is the wrong word (so is shy) but I'll leave it at that.

He turns back, pouting, and then winks at me as a kind of softening of it. Perhaps it's just a twitch. He thinks, if he thinks of me at all: What can she say and what can I say talking to her? What can she possibly know that I don't know already? And so he duck-walks, knock-kneed, out the door.

And now the day begins.

There are really quite a number of things that I can do. I often spend time in the park. Sometimes I rent a boat there and row myself about and feed the ducks. I love museums and there are all those free art galleries and there's window-shopping and if I'm very careful with my budget, now and then I can squeeze in a matinee. But I don't like to be out after Mr. Morrison comes back. I wonder if he keeps his room locked while he's off at work.

His room is directly over mine and he's too big to be a quiet man. The house groans with him and settles when he steps out of bed. The floor creaks under his feet. Even the side walls rustle and the wallpaper clicks its dried paste. But don't think I'm complaining of the noise. I keep track of him this way. Sometimes, here underneath, I ape his movements, bed to dresser, step, clump, dresser to closet and back again. I imagine him there, flat-footed. Imagine him. Just imagine those great legs sliding into pants, their godlike width (for no mere man could have legs like that), those Thor legs into pants holes wide as caves. Imagine those two landscapes, sparsely fuzzed in a faint, wheat-colored brush, finding their way blindly into the waist-wide skirt-things of brown wool that are still damp from yesterday. Ooo. Ugh. Up go the suspenders. I think I can hear him breathe from here.

I can comb my hair three times to his once and I can be out

and waiting at the bottom step by the time he opens his door. "I'm setting my clock by you, Mr. M."

"No time. No time. I'm off. Well . . ." and he shuts the front door so gently one would think he is afraid of his own fat hands.

And so, as I said, the day begins.

The question is (and perhaps it is the question for today): Who is he really, one of the Normals or one of the Others? It's not going to be so easy to find out with someone so fat. I wonder if I'm up to it. Still, I'm willing to go to certain lengths and I'm nimble yet. All that rowing and all that walking up and down and then, recently, I've spent all night huddled under a bush in Central Park and twice I've crawled out on the fire escape and climbed to the roof and back again (but I haven't seen much and I can't be sure of the Others yet).

I don't think the closet will do because there's no keyhole, though I could open the door a crack and maybe wedge my shoe there. (It's double A.) He might not notice it. Or there's the bed to get under. While it's true that I am thin and small, almost child-sized, one might say, still it will not be so easy, but then neither has it been easy to look for lovers on the roof.

Sometimes I wish I were a little, fast-moving lizard, dull green or a yellowish brown. I could scamper in under his stomach when he opened the door and he'd never see me though his eyes are as quick as his feet are clumsy. Still I would be quicker. I would skitter off behind the bookcase or back of his desk or maybe even just lie very still in a corner, for surely he does not see the floor so much. His room is no larger than mine and his presence must fill it, or rather his stomach fills it and his giant legs. He sees the ceiling and the pictures on the wall, the surfaces of night table, desk and bureau, but the floor and the lower halves of every-thing would be safe for me. No, I won't even have to regret not being a lizard, except for getting in. But if he doesn't lock his room it will be no problem and I can spend all day scouting out my hiding places. I'd best take a snack with me, too, if I decide this is the night for it. No crackers and no nuts, but noiseless things like cheese and fig newtons.

It seems to me, now that I think about it, that I was rather saving Mr. Morrison for last, as a child saves the frosting of the cake to eat after the cake part is finished. But I see that I have been foolish for, since he is really one of the most likely prospects, he should have been first.

And so today the day begins with a gathering of supplies and an exploratory trip upstairs.

The room is cluttered. There is no bookcase but there are books and magazines by the hundreds. I check behind the piles. I check the closet, full of drooping, giant suit coats I can easily hide in. Just see how the shoulders extend over the ordinary hangers. I check under the bed and the knee hole of the desk. I squat under the night table. I nestle among the dirty shirts and socks tossed in the corner. Oh, it's better than Central Park for hiding places. I decide to use them all.

There's something very nice about being here for I do like Mr. Morrison. Even just his size is comforting for he's big enough to be everybody's father. His room reassures with all his father-sized things in it. I feel lazy and young here.

I eat a few fig newtons while I sit on his shoes in the closet, soft, wide shoes with their edges all collapsed and all of them shaped more like cushions than shoes. Then I take a nap in the dirty shirts. It looks like fifteen or so but there are only seven and some socks. After that I hunch down in the knee hole of the desk, hugging my knees, and I wait and I begin to have doubts. That pendulous stomach, I can already tell, will be larger than all my expectations. There will certainly be nothing it cannot overshadow or conceal, so why do I crouch here clicking my fingernails against the desk leg when I might be out feeding pigeons? "Leave now," I tell myself. "Are you actually going to spend the whole day, and maybe night, too, cramped and confined in here?" Yet haven't I done it plenty of times lately and always for nothing, too? Why not one more try? for Mr. Morrison is surely the most promising of all. His eyes, the way the fat pushes up his cheeks under them, look almost Chinese. His nose is Roman and in an ordinary face it would be overpowering, but here it is lost. Dwarfed. "Save me," cries the nose. "I'm sinking." I would try, but I will have other, more important duties, after Mr. Morrison comes back, than to save his nose. Duty it is, too, for the good of all and I do mean all. Do not think that I am the least bit prejudiced in this.

You see, I *did* go to a matinee a few weeks ago. I saw the Royal Ballet dance *The Rite of Spring* and it occurred to me then . . . Well, what would *you* think if you saw them wearing their suits that were supposed to be bare skin? Naked suits, I called them. And all those well-dressed, cultured people clapping at them, accepting even though they knew perfectly well . . . like a sort of Emperor's New Clothes in reverse. Now just think, there are only two sexes and every one of us *is* one of those and certainly, presumably that is, knows something of the other. But then that may be where I have been making my mistake. You'd think . . . why, just what I did start thinking, that there must be Others among us.

But it is not out of fear or disgust that I am looking for them. I am open and unprejudiced. You can see that I am when I say that I've never seen (and doesn't this seem strange?) the very organs of my own conception, neither my father's nor my mother's. Goodness knows what *they* were and what this might make me.

So I wait here, tapping my toes inside my slippers and chewing hangnails off my fingers. I contemplate the unvarnished underside of the desk top. I ridge it with my thumbnail. I eat more cookies and think whether I should make his bed for him or not but decide not to. I suck my arm until it is red in the soft crook opposite the elbow. Time jerks ahead as slowly as a school clock, and I crawl across the floor and stretch out behind the books and magazines. I read first paragraphs of dozens of them. What with the dust back here and lying in the shirts and socks before, I'm getting a certain smell and a sort of gray, animal fuzz that makes me feel safer, as though I really did belong in this room and could actually creep around and not be noticed by Mr. Morrison at all except perhaps for a pat on the head as I pass him.

Thump . . . pause. Clump . . . pause. One can't miss his step. The house shouts his presence. The floors wake up squeaking and lean toward the stairway. The banister slides away from his slippery ham-hands. The wallpaper seems suddenly full of bugs. He thinks (if he thinks of me at all): Well, this time she isn't peeking out of her doorway at me. A relief. I can concentrate completely on climbing up. Lift the legs against the pressure. Ooo. Ump. Pause and seem to be looking at the picture on the wall.

I skitter back under the desk.

It's strange that the first thing he does is to put his newspaper on the desk and sit down with his knees next to my nose, regular walls, furnaces of knees, exuding heat and dampness, throwing off a miasma, delicately scented, of wet wool and sweat. What a wide roundness they have to them, those knees. Mother's breasts pressing toward me. Probably as soft. Why can't I put my cheek against them? Observe how he can sit so still with no toe-tapping, no rhythmic tensing of the thigh. He's not like the rest of us, but could a man like this do *little* things?

How the circumstantial evidence piles up, but that is all I've had so far and it is time for something concrete. One thing, just one fact is all I need.

He reads and adjusts the clothing at his crotch and reads again. He breathes out winds of sausages and garlic and I remember that it's after supper and I take out my cheese and eat it as slowly as possible in little rabbit bites. I make a little piece last half an hour.

At last he goes down the hall to the bathroom and I shift back under the shirts and socks and stretch my legs. What if he undresses like my mother did, under a nightgown? under, for him, some giant, double-bed-sized thing?

But he doesn't. He hangs his coat on the little hanger and his tie on the closet doorknob. I receive his shirt and have to make myself another spy hole. Then off with the tortured shoes, then socks. Off come the huge pants with slow, unseeing effort (he stares out the window). He begins on his yellowed undershorts, scratching himself first behind and starting earthquakes across his buttocks.

Where could he have bought those elephantine undershorts? In what store were they once folded on the shelf? In what factory did women sit at sewing machines and put out one after another after another of those otherworldly items? Mars? Venus? Saturn more likely. Or perhaps, instead, a tiny place, some moon of Jupiter with less air per square inch upon the skin and less gravity, where Mr. Morrison can take the stairs three at a time and jump the fences (for surely he's not particularly old) and dance all night with girls his own size.

He squints his Oriental eyes toward the ceiling light and takes off the shorts, lets them fall loosely to the floor. I see Alleghenies of thigh and buttock. How does a man like that stand naked before even a small-sized mirror? I lose myself, hypnotized. Impossible to tell the color of his skin, just as it is with blue-gray eyes or the ocean. How tan, pink, olive and red and sometimes a bruised elephant-gray. His eyes must be used to multiplicities like this, and to plethoras, conglomerations, to an opulence of self, to an intemperate exuberance, to the universal, the astronomical.

I find myself completely tamed. I lie in my cocoon of shirts not even shivering. My eyes do not take in what they see. He is utterly beyond my comprehension. Can you imagine how thin my wrists must seem to him? He is thinking (if he thinks of me at all), he thinks: She might be from another world. How alien her ankles and leg bones. How her eyes do stand out. How green her complexion in the shadows at the edges of her face (for I must admit that perhaps I may be as far along the scale at my end of "humanity" as he is at his).

Suddenly I feel like singing. My breath purrs in my throat in hymns as slow as Mr. Morrison himself would sing. Can this be love? I wonder. My first *real* love? But haven't I always been passionately interested in people? Or rather in those who caught my fancy? But isn't this feeling entirely different? Can love really have come to me this late in life? (La, la, lee la, from whom all blessings flow . . .) I shut my eyes and duck my head into the shirts. I grin into the dirty socks. Can you imagine *him* making love to *me!*

Well below his abstracted, ceilingward gaze, I crawl on elbows and knees back behind the old books. A safer place to shake out the silliness. Why, I'm old enough for him to be (had I ever married) my youngest son of all. Yet if he were a son of mine, how he would have grown beyond me. I see that I cannot ever follow him (as with all sons). I must love him as a mouse might love the hand that cleans the cage, and as uncomprehendingly, too, for surely I see only a part of him here. I sense more. I sense deeper largenesses. I sense excesses of bulk I cannot yet imagine. Rounded afterimages linger on my eyeballs. There seems to be a mysterious darkness in the corners of the room and his shadow covers, at the same time, the window on one wall and the mirror on the other. Certainly he is like an iceberg, seven-eighths submerged.

But now he has turned toward me. I peep from the books, holding a magazine over my head as one does when it rains. I do so more to shield myself from too much of him all at once than to hide.

And there we are, confronting each other eye to eye. We stare and he cannot seem to comprehend me any more than I can comprehend him, and yet usually, it seems, his mind is ahead of mine, jumping away on unfinished phrases. His eyes are not even wistful and not yet surprised. But his belly button . . . here is the eye of God at last. It nestles in a vast, bland sky like a sun on the curve of the universe flashing me a wink of heat, a benign, fat wink. The stomach eye accepts and understands. The stomach eye recognizes me and looks at me as I've always wished to be looked at. (Yea, though I walk through the valley of the shadow of death.) I see you now.

But I see him now. The skin hangs in loose, plastic folds just there, and there is a little copper-colored circle like a quarter made out of pennies. There's a hole in the center and it is corroded green at the edges. This must be a kind of "naked suit" and whatever the sex organs may be, they are hidden behind this hot, pocked and pitted imitation skin.

I look into those girlish eyes of his and there is a big nothing, as blank as though the eyeballs are all whites . . . as blank as having no sex at all . . . like being built like a boy doll with a round hole for the water to empty out (something to frighten little-boy three-year-olds).

God, I think. I am not religious but I think: My God, and then I stand up and somehow, in a limping run, I get out of there and down the stairs as though I fly. I slam the door of my room and slide in under my bed. The most obvious of hiding places, but after I am there I can't bear to move out. I lie and listen for his thunder on the stairs, the roar of his feet splintering the steps, his hand tossing away the banister as he comes like an engulfing wave.

I know what I'll say. "We accept. We accept," I'll say. "We will love" (I love already) "whatever you are."

I lie listening, watching the hanging edges of my bedspread in the absolute silence of the house. Can there be anyone here at all in such a strange quietness? Must I doubt even my own existence?

"Goodness knows," I'll say, "if I'm a Normal myself." (How is one to know such things when everything is hidden?) "Tell all of them that we accept. Tell them it's the naked suits that are ugly. Tell them the truth is beautiful. Your dingles, your dangles, wrinkles, ruts, bumps and humps, we accept. (We will love.) Your loops, strings, worms, buttons, figs, cherries, flower petals, your soft little toad shapes, warty and greenish, your cats' tongues and rats' tails, your oysters, one-eyed between your legs, garter snakes, snails, we accept. (Isn't the truth always more lovable?)

But what a long silence this is. Where is he? For he must (mustn't he?) come after me for what I saw. If there has been all this hiding and if he must wear that cache sex thing across his front, then he *must* silence me somehow, destroy me even. But where is he? Perhaps he thinks I've locked my door. But I haven't. I haven't.

Why doesn't he come?

Dog Is Dead

The matador has changed costume. Now he wears white silk with gold braid. He stands in the center of the arena.

"Let the moon make the first move, Veronica."

Once, Veronica, running toward him wearing her yellow dress, looked like springtime when it was already October.

He waved to her over his newspaper and she ran on past. She had not seen him. Perhaps had not seen him. She might not have noticed him there, half covered by newspapers, where he had spent the afternoon watching people make love one way or another and in unlikely positions, his face turned from them, watching out of the corner of his eye. Perhaps she had not seen him except out of the corner of her eye as she ran on past that day wearing a yellow dress, but now he might lie under the bench instead of on it, and it is more likely he would count flies, dragon-flies, having grown near-sighted. Would she notice him? Newspaper on stomach? His name is Nat. "Hello, Veronica," but she ran on past.

He is thinking of all the things that can be touched, such as skin, scales, fly's wing, oyster, eyeball, chicken feet, breasts and walnuts. Thinking: Nat and Veronica in the garden, in the bathtub, in the closet, in an old trunk, in the vestibule, running toward

him in a yellow dress, holding up two fingers in some sign he
has heard the meaning of once but has forgotten. Thinks (remembering the sign): That great cow was once queen of everything. And I will be the swan king, he thinks, and sit by the
pool while Veronica sings, wondering: Anybody coming two by
two yet? And: Are there any lovers needing encouragement? It's
my hand to help them on their way. Nat, with a daisy in his
lapel, hat over his eyes, pin-stripe suit, thinks: I will keep them
from giving up too soon. I will supply an incentive, lend them
lubricants and comfort and know-how. Thinks: I will kick
them on their way and lick them on their way and kick them out
when it's over, Nat matador, all in green satin this time, with the
moon looking like a fingernail paring. Some say, "Dog is dead and
Nat is under park benches again," but he says, "Nat is remembering. Nat is facing his problems as a flower faces the sun," and as a
flower faces the sun, so Veronica turns toward the moon. Yellow
dress seems white in this light. Turn around but don't make any
unnecessary moves, Nat is telling himself, and: Remember, it's
the free season, maybe time for the earliest clarinet of all and
Veronica is singing and walking in a dignified way while some
people stay in the park all night long even if the gates are locked
at midnight, or because they are locked or, even if they are locked
out, somehow they get in and are in there with Nat, maybe even
in the park now with Nat who is always wearing a green tie in
this weather with this sweater and with the moonish moon. He
has been constipated for three days and thinks: One day I will
lay the world itself as white as an egg, but it is Veronica, queen
of the sea or of a tree who has the pregnant belly that is not really
pregnant but only seems so, for Nat has not yet touched Veronica
as if to touch an oyster or fly's wing or eyeball. Here she comes
now, but it isn't the middle of the night anymore. Only noon.
No moon. Nat waves to her vaguely. Perhaps he's brushing at a
fly on his *New York Times.* Perhaps she doesn't see him, or sees
him but doesn't remember who he is. Her fingers make a sign,
either consciously or unconsciously, that he has forgotten the

meaning of. Should he get up and follow her? Veronica and Nat, then, would be someplace together. Nat and Veronica in the herb garden or under the lilacs or someplace in between, or on the very bench where he sits and reads.

But what if the swan king finds himself knee deep in the pond reaching for bread crumbs. Just so, out of the medium comes the thought as out of the water comes the bread to the beak of the swan or the hand of a man who has become a little bit too bald. Yesterday his face was pure. Now he knows (or suspects) all his own faults and his own fault and maybe how it happened that he should have followed her.

He thinks that he should never appear before her (or any of them) except all in white and on Saturdays he would wear a gold ring on his thumb. This might seem feminine but to Veronica being a woman is something she does every day. Her daily endeavor. It has to do with running through the park in a yellow dress and singing her songs or a particular song. It has to do with hair, with lips, with hips, and with the birth of love or of love's longing or of something simpler than love.

And what if a frog plops into the pond? What if Nat watches a wild goose fly by? Should he follow her? In the face of possible sore feet and bramble bushes and in spite of not remembering what the sign means and the endless possibilities of rejection? And what if she was motioning to the man behind him, if there was a man behind him, which there might very well have been? There might have been a man behind him that he hadn't noticed just walking by at that moment. There might have been a dog or an old lady or a bird or a cat or a bullfrog in this weather and at this time of day there might have been any of these. At any given moment there might be any of these or a big man behind him with some weapon. Especially at night. Perhaps a handsome man. So that when the swan king makes his entrance into the park, timing it to coincide with the coming of sparrows, he may run across some drum major he hasn't bargained for and other surprises, and yet what if he confines himself to the park and to one bar on Front Street?

Meanwhile he has spelled out VERONICA in little white stones in the pansy bed, thinking: But if you think I'm not the god of one kind of desire or hopefulness or hopeless here in the flesh in this park by moonlight on the bench after the gates are locked . . . if you think I'm not something still uncatalogued by science or anything else, then let the pigeons all fly away from me with the coo of mourning doves and let me lose the walnut in my pocket, and if you can say, any more than I can say, that you understand the motives behind this desire, which I might say might have been caused by thus and thus and yet when I think of possible reasons I still can't be sure which, if any of them, is the true reason, or which one or two *the* one or two reasons or even three reasons for this desire, so that I might be forever mistaken about myself just as you might be forever mistaken about me, never able to judge properly at all but only to present possibilities and yet all of us knowing that Nat could follow Veronica even without some reason for it. Except that she has passed him by, red cloak and all, and not answered his greeting. "Hello, Veronica," he said, but she ran on past and now he only seems to brush a fly from his *New York Times* and reads that the temperature may dip to fifty-five. New moon on the twenty-seventh. Monday night. After hours. Park waking up now. This is the real beginning, in the moonlight, of all he's ever thought of. In the center of the arena the matador (after hours for him, too). In the center of the arena, in the moonlight now because it's later than it was. Now he wears a pin-stripe suit, a green striped tie and a shirt with a dirty collar and waits for someone else to make the first move. This is the real beginning, he thinks. Here. Motionless. The motionless beginning. The wind has died. Only the moon moves and VERONICA is written in white pebbles not far from where he stands. How long can he go on like this with no other reason except for the one right now and no other season but this one, a season for bullfrogs, and a reason to follow her in spite of a sign or because of a sign she is making with her fingers? What if Nat were transferred into the sky so that the moon might be his real antagonist and the sun become someone of whom he could say "I see myself in that man," and then, if his name should be reversed, it could be said, as in syllogisms, all Dog is Nat, Tan is Nat, man is Tan and therefore Dog is man. Nat is thinking: If I could make it happen. Take off my hat and tie and make it come true.

Ducklike the swan king moves toward his goal. His bullfrog swallowed whole. Bullfights over now. In the center of the arena earth mother, Veronica, spreads her legs but not for him. Nat waits, watching from the corner of his eye, wondering if this is the right season or reason. Only the moon moves. It is time for a philosophical view of life. One that has elegance and symmetry. Time for a view of the world that's as pale as the moon. Matador, natador, it's the drum major that this place belongs to after all, unless maybe the moon comes out at noon. Some say, "Dog is dead and Nat does not yet follow Veronica into some sunset or other" (and would some ever say, "Nat is Dog"?), but Dog lies in his own diarrhea . . . his last dying diarrhea and for Nat it is the real beginning.

Nothing moves.

Moon.

I Love You

In a dream I follow him to a cocktail party full of his admirers. I am three steps behind like a Japanese wife, my skirt too tight so I have to trot, my bra strap coming down. Perhaps the whole thing is undone. It really happened like this, or almost, and I was left in a dirty hallway. The door slammed shut before I could get my toe in and he had forgotten about me already. I sat on the steps in my new coat, my new dress, and I only dreamed it after it had already come true.

In another dream I have slipped on the ice and chipped my knee. I feel like a violinist who has lost his bow but I really don't have a violin anymore now. We sold it to buy a motorcycle the week after we were married, BSA, 500 cc, eighty miles per gallon. The violin was a Kloz, 1767.

Yesterday I almost walked into the side of a speeding Karmann Ghia, a red one on Fourteenth Street, and I knew then I would have a bad dream. I didn't tell him about it when I got home. I was thinking that if my name were Maya or Miranda or Dido or Sonja, and if I had long hair and an ability to tell fortunes, I would pick the queen of swords for myself and lay out seven cards, but instead I opened the Bible at random. I shut my eyes and let some force take over my finger. Ruth, of course, chapter 4, verse 4. It says: "And I thought to advertise thee, saying, Buy it before the inhabitants, and before the elders of my people." I had expected something poetic and full of ancient wisdom. "Buy it" isn't "Love it." I keep wondering, what can this mean?

My grandmother worshiped a god's naked son and when her finger moved it touched the right word every time. (If I had been fighting with my brothers she found: "Surely the churning of milk bringeth forth butter, and the wringing of the nose bringeth forth blood." Proverbs, chapter 30, verse 33.)

How dirty my coat is getting on these stairs. They aren't keeping their hallways clean here. Cats are at the window. Gray cats at gray windows are invisible. Background gray. Air gray. I might stage this and dance it someday. *Memories of Husbands Waited For.* Gray masks. Gray leotards and tights. Graying hair. My stockings down around my ankles. A red X marks the spot where I am supposed to be and where I am. Gray ocean. Gray sky. Gray beach. Red X. My new coat is gray, too. (How could I have bought a coat the color of this hall!) If he has really forgotten about me he will go home some back way, thinking I will be there to unlock the door. He will remember being admired and tell me about it while I heat up clam juice and answer, Yes, yes.

Once I waited for you in a Spanish desert beside a road measured out by rulers to the horizon line while you walked away. Dry Kansas-large fields, no place to get out of the sun, only a shallow roadside ditch I dared to pee in after the first hour of waiting while you went to get something to patch a tire. It's good no one passed by that day because I've heard since that people sometimes disappear in Spain, gone without a trace (motorcycle and all probably), and no one ever hears of them again.

I'm trying to have a good attitude. I shut my eyes and think: This *is* a sad-looking beach. Only the sound of a cat, no surf, no shells, no driftwood, a few cigarette butts. I open my eyes and take off my shoes. The heels will make good hammers or good weapons. I think I hear dancing in there and I know Maya is in the apartment. She was once a very beautiful woman. He and I and Maya (and almost everyone else we know) are at the age when men become more desirable and women less so. I used to have a violin teacher at the desirable age for men and once he chased me around the Ping-Pong table of the recreation room at music camp. Lessons were never the same after that. I didn't even want him to push on my elbow (whole bow), flatten my wrist or bend the first joint of my little finger to the proper curve, but I was in love with him. He was very intense, very Viennese and had a Russian accent.

But this isn't dirt from sitting on the steps, not all of it. More likely the menstrual five days early. Unprepared. Improvise. Sit on it. Silk is not absorbent. My mother was prepared. I think she must have watched my underpants every day for half a year when my breasts began to grow, waiting till she had to tell me what she didn't want to talk about at all. How else could she have caught it so cleverly at just the right time? I thought she was going to punish me for soiling my pajamas, but she showed me how to put on the waistband and pads. She looked sullen but I suppose she was just embarrassed.

This happened before I entered the conservatory and fractured my kneecap falling on the stairs the time my violin teacher almost caught me. It is incredible to me to think of any woman not being in love with my violin teacher. (Probably my mother was in love with him, too.) He was quite well known in music circles and played with a major orchestra. My mother was paying a lot for those lessons. I didn't dare not go, but I tried to keep the music stand between us and I blushed a lot. He was sympathetic about the chipped kneecap and sent me a box of fudge his wife had made.

Agnes, Alice, Anita, Candida, Cleo . . . on to Yvonne, Zenia, Zoe. Come out now. I know you're in there. I don't care if the young men crowd up. And who helped you? the famous advice-giver to the younger men? Sometimes *I* did. I still do. You remind me of my violin teacher, quite well known in your own circles, except there's one difference. Is it because I'm no longer sixteen? But I have married you before I knew enough to ask some token, something as precious as blood.

There you are, Antonin Artaud haircuts for men your age who are balding in front, coats, pants, socks, underwear to match the haircut. You're neither Viennese nor intense, rather a dirty Parisian gray as though the baths were still even here sixty cents apiece, but, looking again, I see this is an oily beach. One can't help the dirt. Once we swam here and came out with orange peels in our hair, coffee grounds between our toes. I waited for you to get tired of martinis that day, too, and before then tired of the waves and grapefruit rinds, and I worried that the tide had taken you beyond the swimming area and that you were much too far out.

The longer I sit the more it flows. I have been here since twilight or dawn. I should have brought a beach basket of supplies, lipstick, eye shadow, nail files, potato chips. By now I will have to stay here until the wind dries me off. Silk is sticky and slippery. Green mixed with red becomes black.

At a party in honor of him at a castle once, the steps had thick carpeting. I went to sleep on them descending to the dining room. They were wide as a bed, red quilted. The face of a great man (or a rich man) hung at the landing, swords, kings' crowns, flags, men's things for decorations all around. I could have been raped on that stairway but he was in the lecture hall, everyone listening to him. They didn't hear me cry out. But this isn't that kind of party at all. The talk is the same, but the cookies are full of pot. Maya baked them. She knows where I am. I sit here still trying to have a good attitude. Be mature, I tell myself. Smoke a cigarette butt swept out from the apartment next door. Count roaches. Come to realize that my dress is no longer new.

Sit in the menstrual hut until it's over while he's out hunting with the other men. Spear and arrow club by special invitation only. Tie, jacket, but any haircut. Beards. I live in this hall. I'm beginning to recognize it from before. I've seen it in my mother's eyes. (I will tell my daughter a different story. I'll say, Ask your husband for something as precious as blood.)

Perhaps five old men live across from Maya's place and take turns looking out the keyhole at me. They may also spy through holes in the bathroom wall they have chinked out with screwdrivers. (Mother thought gas station rest rooms were full of eye holes like that.)

Get up. Give them a show, stockings falling down or not. There's plenty of music. Always plenty of music, rum-de-dum, or make up your own. *Husband's Waiting Dance* will be too slow for them.

I dared him to enter the menstrual hut and face the demons, but even the younger men won't go near it. My husband and all my brothers are six feet tall and have other places they dare go. Imagine in the summer cottage no bigger than menstrual hut, the four people six feet tall and then me, as though the female were another race entirely. Everyone of them had a plaid wool shirt that year. I did, too. In those days I wasn't any particular sex at all, except they never minded the cold as I did. This time of year the beach is icy. Empty. Yellow sand with black ridges. No shells. Nothing to pick up here. Cats that sound like sea gulls.

"Buy it," the Bible said, and "I had thought to advertise thee," but now must I advertise myself? Oh, I do advertise *him*. I always have. (My violin teacher was advertised already.) What if I advertise myself and if I go in with beach things? clams, cold French fries, cigarette butts. What they will think is salt is really sand and the lox is mackerel. The cats won't eat it. You have already stuffed them with chopped liver.

I get up and hop a bit to warm myself. If you come for me, I'll be dancing. I'll have you sit on the stairs in your good suit and wait till you shit in your pants. Only then can we go home together in some kind of mutual understanding.

But Maya's door opens and here he comes now, a little drunk, with Shirley, Helena, Miranda, Sonja. As usual, he is looking at the ceiling and doesn't see me. Shirley, Helena, Miranda and Sonja look at me as though they remember having seen me somewhere before but they don't remember that I'm his wife. They never do, but then he often forgets to introduce me. There he goes, followed by the shorter men. If I hurry home I can be there before he is and I can unlock the door for him just as he expects me to. I know I can beat him back, because he will be taking them out for coffee.

All that about the menstrual was just anxiety, so if I can keep a good attitude and smile when he comes in maybe he'll make love to me tonight.

Peninsula

Do you realize we are all connected by telephone wires? I do not mean that our voices go through the wires to each other, though, of course, that is true, but that we are *physically* connected by the wires we talk through. We are actually physically wired to every house with a telephone as though there were a roadway set out for wingless birds. Except for the underground wires in some cities, a bird could walk from a house in New York to one in California, so, when we speak to someone, no matter how far away, we are wired, literally, ear to ear. We are connected, we are touching through wires, across whatever distance.

I think this is a wonderful thing to contemplate. Imagine the freedom of the tightrope walkers.

I have just recently begun to think about this. This is such a large house to be alone in that I do like the idea of the telephone wires, even when one is not talking through them, still being connected to all the houses, for one can't see a single building or sign of life from here (here, where there used to be so much life). From as high as the attic windows, there is only a glimpse or two of the sound, so if I should put my hand upon the wires, I would be in the only possible contact with life that I can manage, but it would be a contact actually more physically close than that of eyes or ears.

The telephone wire leaves this house just below an attic window, about fifteen inches under it, to be exact. After leaving the house, the wire goes out to a cross-shaped pole, the lower half of which is hidden in lilac bushes that are in bloom now. There is a thin wire out of each end of the crosspiece as though out of a hand, wires that stretch away to the south toward a neck of land where they cross, along with the road, to the mainland. Lower, on the body of the pole itself, there is one thicker wire, also leading south.

This morning I decided to make a bed up here in the attic next to this little window. I wanted to be closer to the wires, not the telephones. In fact, since the calls yesterday, I would like to get away from the telephones altogether. I like the idea that the wires are connected to everyone regardless if one is talking through them or not, but actual telephone conversations can sometimes be quite distressing.

I feel comfortable up here looking out at where the birds sit along the wires and I have found myself a nice bed. It is narrow, white-painted and youth-sized. Though I am not very large for a grown-up person, I cannot quite straighten out in it, but this bed, I knew, would be easier for me to set up and besides, I like it. There is no reason now for me not to have what I like and I do not mind in the least not being able to stretch out completely.

Sitting on the bed and looking out at the wires, I wonder, where have all the others gone, all those I loved so, and how have I failed them? I wonder, was I too young? Did I marry before I was ready? What made them all disappear so suddenly, so cruelly? But then perhaps it wasn't my fault. Perhaps they had some accident that wiped them all out silently and quickly, every one of them, before I was aware that they were gone at all, or perhaps someone came at midnight and murdered them all while they were stretched out, vulnerable, upon their beds. Or perhaps it is I, after all, that they have murdered. Yes, they have left me half dead here, all of them driving away over the gravel that sounded like ice as they left. They have murdered me with their backs turned, taking away even the little black dog that was mine, taking away the setter that was his, and the hound, and the two myna birds, and every small bit of life except these wild birds that sit so blackly upon the wires and that have never belonged to anyone.

But this place is not an island. (I insist it is not though some called it that.) I, too, can leave. I can walk away from this fist-shaped peninsula anytime I wish and go south, for the river does not flow across that whole wrist of land, but comes from some inland source. I can go south, then, by way of the road, or by the stepping stones of the river, or along the telephone wires like my wingless birds. Ah, but these birds that sit like little lady's shoes along the wires, of course, *have* wings and do not really need the wires at all. It is I who am wingless. But do acrobats need wings when they step out on their wires and am I any less than they, I who used to dance balanced on my toes?

While sitting here looking out, I have a lovely thought. I think that all the acrobats of the world come out at night upon the telephone wires (who can say they don't?), the girls with pink parasols for balancing and the boys with white poles. The boys wear tights and colored vests and the girls have short skirts and flowery hats. They ask each other, "Going south for Carnival?" when they meet, and many of them most certainly must answer, Yes. I would like to see them when night comes. I would like to see them shining silvery in the moonlight. I would like to join them there.

How quiet the house is when it used to be so full of chatter. Now if the telephone rings, it points out the silence with exclamations, frames it into isolated sections of nothingness. Actually there are four telephones here; some ring in unison and some independently. There's the downstairs phone, the upstairs phone, the maid's phone and his telephone, the one he carried with him and plugged in wherever he was. That one is still on the side porch where the sun warms it in the mornings and warms the chair beside it. I sat in that chair yesterday. The cushion was uncomfortably hot. I wonder how he could have sat there so often. Yet the sun would have been absorbed down into his bones. He would have been only pleasantly warm, as though more alive than the rest of us.

It was then, as I sat there, that the phone first rang, his phone, and I answered it. I don't think that it was a random call, that someone just got this number by accident as they dialed whatever fell under their fingers. This is an unlisted phone and not many people know the number. "Is this 516-275-6634?" the person asked. "Is it . . .?" he said and mentioned my name. Why, I wonder, did I ever say, "Yes, this is . . ." and that name?

The man at the police station to whom I spoke directly afterward said that this sort of call was not infrequent. "We get complaints of this sort every day," he said, "but a fellow like that usually gets all his kicks by telephone. He won't come by. They never do." "But it was awful." I said. "I never heard such language. I couldn't repeat to you the words he used and the things he said he wanted to be doing with me, my whole body, and speaking of love to me in those words, those awful words. I'm alone here," I said. "I'm all alone here now." That was the first I had told anyone that they all were gone . . . Mother, Father, little brother . . .

I brought my family with me when I married. There was more than enough room. We were passionately happy. I was daughter, sister, wife and mother all in one and even to this very ornamental house I was an additional ornament. I sat in the alcove next to the bird cages dressed in silk chiffon. I strolled the living room in a black mantilla. I still do. I languished by the garden doors in green brocade. I waited up and down the hallway in a little feathered hat that, like the neck of a mallard, was one color in the shadows and another in the light. I leaned at porch screens until my forehead was cross-hatched. I pulled back the curtains at the windows and looked out at the rain or, as the case might be, the sunshine. I still do. In fact, yesterday I looked out upon the wind and sun.

Strange how things happen. One can see a pattern forming in the events that have occurred these last days. There is an odd significance beginning to make itself felt and I must stay open to it. I must understand it when it has finished unfolding itself to me. I see that now, and that I must put together each incident to form a whole. I must not look at things separately.

Yesterday I woke to such a white morning light and I went out for the first time in . . . I don't really remember when. I don't remember dressing. I must have still worn whatever I wore to bed. There, in the woods that surround this house, I ran for the sheer joy of moving. I ran, but I stayed away from the sound, for I did not want to hear the stones upon the beach, all those washed-white, bony stones sifting with a hollow rustle. The largest lie in a stripe quite a few feet from the water, a stripe, east, north and west. Imagine it, this line of larger pebbles marking out this land on three sides. One cannot know its meaning, but notice that yesterday everything started with a vast, white light.

I ran then, as though pursued by the morning sky. I ran, ran, ran until the sun came up completely and then I turned south toward the river, to the grassy hollow where we made love once. How we did make love in all the crooks and hollows of this place he called an island. If there ever was a difference between us, that was certainly the only one, whether this was an island or not, for he could seem as young as I was.

But if I stopped there to rest a moment, it wasn't because of that memory of lovemaking, but because I could see across the little river and I could see the stepping stones, one before the other. I could see the evidence of the rightness of my point of view and I could see the road to my release. But something stopped me from crossing then, as though, even before the pattern became apparent, before there *was* such a thing as a pattern, I, somehow, wanted to stay to see it unfold itself.

Standing there, not because we once made love there, yet remembering that lovemaking time, I wondered if my faun-brown brother could have been hiding in the weeds and wild flowers then, peering down at us from Queen Anne's lace, seeing me with my skirts around my waist. He could well have seen us for he was always in the woods, my stealthy brother, my little animal creature who had never had a beach or a forest of his own before and yet who became a part of them so quickly. He had never grown so thin and tall. How old was that brother of mine, I wonder, twelve or sixteen? A graceful age, at least, all legs, all knuckles. Sometimes it seemed I saw him in a mirror and he was my other, my male, self, my face atop his bony body, the real me, and never had I been so lovable as in him as he walked barefoot in the woods or came inside the house bringing the smell of the woods with him.

We made love there, he (not my brother) and I, and he said to me then that he could not read my smile, could not fathom what it meant, and yet, he said, "I can see that there is some meaning to it. But, anyway, I'm glad you smile," he said. And why was I smiling? Was I thinking that if this place was really an island, we could have monkeys and let them swing, wild, in the trees and if it was not an island, they would get away, but if it was, then they would stay? Or could I have been remembering all the scarfs he had bought me and my shelf of hats?

But I can't really remember that smile of mine at all. I can remember yesterday when I came back hungry for breakfast after all that running and found a little dead mouse on the kitchen floor, just an ordinary little brown mouse in the middle of the bright tan tiles, looking more incongruous than it might have looked because the kitchen was all done over so recently in whites and browns.

I picked the mouse up on the edge of a newspaper, using a stick to push it for I could not bear to touch it with my hands, and I put it in the garbage. Of what significance can a little dead mouse be? I must have asked myself then, or rather, I could not have even thought about it at all, since I was not yet aware of any of these patterns. Then I was only conscious of being alone and of having been alone for some specified length of time but I could not remember how long.

After getting rid of the mouse, I took a cold chicken leg and a hard-boiled egg from the refrigerator for my breakfast. It was already late morning and when I finished I went out on the side porch and sat down. Soon after that there came that first phone call, of which I've already spoken.

He would always answer his phone briskly, not with Hello, but Yes. He never said his name. He never said, This is so-and-so, but, staring at one of us, at me or my brother or one or the other of our twin baby girls sitting up in their twin chairs, staring, it seemed, into our skulls, he said, Buy, or Sell. That was always all there was to it. I had never answered this phone before but I answered it with Hello.

The voice was the same the second time as the first time, but the second call came after my second meal for the day, which was my supper and for which I had exactly what I had had for breakfast. (Notice all these seconds: a second meal, a second call, another egg, a bit of chicken.)

The voice was the same the second time as the first, the same man's voice and the same words, the same obscene talk of love of me. I think only a very fat person could have such a low voice or could speak so thick-tongued and say the words so slowly. He almost had a tune to his talk and a rhythm, as though those awful words were poetry.

I suppose one might ask why I didn't just hang up right away. That's what I ask myself, too. Why did I listen all the way to the end? Even if he rang again after I hung up, I need not have answered, knowing it was he. I certainly would not have thought that it might be one of the family calling me right after his call, regretfully asking my forgiveness or even asking me to come with them, perhaps saying they were all driving back to pick me up. "We wouldn't leave you as though you had died here. We wouldn't leave you isolated. You are too young to be so lonely," they might have said, but it wouldn't have been any of them then and so I really need not have heard any of that fat person's call and I certainly need not have heard the second one, knowing what was coming, and yet, as though hypnotized by the slow rhythms of the words and the whispering quality of the voice, I listened to the end.

After that I called the police again and they were sympathetic but they didn't see what they could do. I talked to the same man as before and his voice was such that I wondered if he, too, hadn't recently lost some loved ones. I, with my own great losses, could understand it in him. I could hear it. Death was in his voice, sad, loving death. He had once been happy, deliriously so, as I had been. "I'll tell the prowl car to drive over there and check around a couple of times tonight if it would make you feel better, but, like I said before, those fellows stick to the phone." "It would make me feel better," I said, not realizing what it would be like to be hearing them drive over the gravel like some of them coming home, not realizing how their red light would flash and how their spot would play upon the house.

At first, last evening, I had lit all the lights, but that made the windows into mirrors and we have too many mirrors as it is, although I did used to like to see myself for I fit in so beautifully with each room no matter how different. Chameleon-like, I seemed biologically adaptable to every décor. Mirrors and reflecting windows seemed to provide me with a black edge as though I were in a picture and the artist had drawn me with more vigor than anything or anyone else in it. My brother was like that, too. We both had an outline that was more than just our black hair and eyes. But last night I went about shutting curtains and avoiding mirrors, for these days I see such an isolated me, a me who wears a strange smile that even I cannot fathom. Did *he* know? Had he guessed something then, and if he were here now could he tell me what he really thought of that smile so that I, too, might get some idea of what it was about? Yet it does seem to me that I used to know what was in my head at those times.

Shutting all the curtains did not help, so I turned off all the lights and opened the curtains again. The moon made enough light for me. Then the mirrors reflected almost blackness except for my moon-colored face, and the windows all looked out again instead of in. I went up to my old bedroom, not up here to the little bed I have set up for myself by the wires, but to my regular room next to his and across from the twins, and there I sat staring at my doorway because I had left my door open into the dark hall and there was such a deep black oblong shape there, as though it came from all the way down two stairways into the cellar. I don't know how long I sat staring, but I heard the police car come. I heard their wheels along the gravel coming slowly and soon I could see the rhythmic reflections of their red light upon my ceiling. I suppose they had turned it on to let me know who they were. At first it made me think of blood and I felt a strange dizziness, but then I realized how gay it really was, like the lights on a Ferris wheel or on top of a carnival booth for shooting little metal foxes that go by one by one.

With these thoughts, the dizziness passed and I went to the window. They were playing their spotlight over the front of the house as though to catch some monkey-man clinging to the walls where there was no place to cling, and then they lit the surfaces of all the bushes along the turnaround. After a few moments they drove away over spitting gravel. I looked out again, farther out into the moonlight, and there were no monkey creatures upon the walls at all and the bushes still hid whatever they had hid before, under the spotlight's eye.

I did not sleep at all that night and I heard them when they came again, flashing their lights in the same way. I knew they would not come after that. I knew this second visit would be the last.

It was in the early morning that I came up here in the attic and got this little bed out, setting it up with the dawn coming through the window, and because there were birds sitting, singing, on the wires, I found I could, at last, go to sleep.

When I awoke much later, there were only two birds left, two gray little things sitting silent and motionless. I saw at once that they were omens. I saw those two birds like a warning of all the duplicates of the day before. I remembered the little brown mouse on the kitchen floor and I was ready as I came downstairs, though not exactly ready for what was there.

How do you suppose that pale and perfect hand, cut off just above the wrist, got upon the Persian rug just inside the living room door? I almost didn't see it except for the warning of the birds. Yet it may have been there all this time and I only just noticed it as I came downstairs, or perhaps it somehow flew in in the night. It lay palm down, poised, like a five-legged spider, a left hand, facing me with the mouth of its wound. It lay very still but it looked as though it were capable of action, the fingers stretched out behind it, relaxed, each one curving so that the tips touched the rug. If this hand were nothing but a finger or perhaps a thumb, it would have lain there utterly inert, or if it were an arm, it would seem unwieldy, incapable of any but dragging movements, but a hand is quite a different thing. This one seemed, resting there five-legged, a study of the principles of motion.

It was familiar to me, a friendly, perhaps beloved hand, but I could not think where I had seen it before or whose it could be. It was like a person whom one cannot remember the name of or exactly where one is used to seeing them, a person met completely out of the usual context. I knew this hand and yet it was certainly not his and I could not even tell for sure which sex it had belonged to.

It has grown late as I sit again upon my little bed thinking: Should I have left it lying there? Haven't I some sort of obligation to it? Some duty I should perform? Certainly I can't put it into the garbage with the mouse. But I have done nothing about it. That hand tells a wordless story, answers all questions if one wished to consider it, to face it. If one could bring oneself to clasp it, perhaps, in order to recognize its touch and thereby the person it once belonged to, one would have the answer to these last days. But I have decided I will not face that hand, for its mouth is too wide. I am sure it tells too much.

Here in this attic it isn't hard to find a pole. I use a long piece of white wood, molding, no doubt, for it is rounded along one edge and square on the other. I lean my head out of the window and listen to the ticking night sounds. I have put on my dancing shoes. I do realize how we are all connected physically by those wires we talk through—a road for wingless birds. Downstairs I hear the faint ringing of some phone or other.

I have decided that I will not think about that hand anymore or about whatever obligations I may have toward it. It is much more interesting to try to understand this slowly revealed pattern of whiteness and twoness, of strange phone calls, lights upon police cars and white, hard-boiled eggs. These are what I will concern myself with, but as a whole, not as isolated incidents. The hand belongs distinctly with the mouse. I must not let myself think of it alone.

In the moonlight outside I see . . . I seem to see a flock of flying fish all silver in the sky, silent as bats, with stiff, serrated wings, double wings like dragonflies, two on each side. Tomorrow they might have had three, but tonight they have two.

I think I am beginning to see the pattern and I am a part of it.

I will step out upon the wire.

No, they have not murdered me, nor I them. I have not, by any chance, cut them up (even to the last myna bird) and hid them in the cellar, nor they me, for I am wholly here and with both my hands upon my long, pale arms.

Carefully I will walk out to the first cross-shaped pole, where the smell of lilac will rise up to me like mist. I can think of myself as miraculously stepping over the crucifixion, Christ hanging there below me, each upper wire at the ends of the crosspiece coming from a palm of his hand and the lower wire piercing his side. He is a lovely, pale and waxy boy, naked in the moonlight, as luminous as one of those fish that passed so silently by. He is quite dead, his head hanging sideways and down, almost as though his neck were broken. He is beardless and his short, black Jewish hair all comes forward, soft as a little cat-skin cap. He looks like one of those acrobat boys that walk the wires at night. All he needs are white tights and a little blue or orange vest. He is smiling. I will step over him on one of the topmost and thinnest wires, lightly as though I needed no wires at all. My pole will balance gently from side to side. I feel young. I *am* young and I am beautiful. I will go south along the treetops.

I step out upon the wire.

Chicken Icarus

I keep thinking there must be some place for me somewhere. I keep thinking of some kind of gelatin land, some puddingy spot all viscous, muculent, where the air is thick and wet as water. I wouldn't even ask to be able to fly around in it. I'd be happy just to ooze along the bottom as long as it was nothing like floors or mattresses or pillows. But the way it is around here you can get pretty bored with gravity.

"Down with downness," I say.

I keep thinking about this sticky-slippery kind of land but I think about legs, too, a lot more than I think about arms. I don't know why. Maybe because I always hear walking sounds. Around the house I hear the floors creak and thump, accepting feet. Outside, the lady's heels tick-tock, tick-tock, measuring out time in distance covered. Steps per minute about sixty-five, breaths twenty, heartbeats seventy-two. It takes me ten heartbeats to cross my mattress. Rolling. Well, more like five heartbeats or four. Four little bird heartbeats. (I exaggerate myself, but sometimes I feel pretty exaggerated.)

Doorknobs, on/off switches, buttons, zippers, drawer pulls, toenail scissors, the little thumbscrews that hold my reading stand, the handles on the sides of my mattress, the armholes of my shirt, even birds . . . When they sit along the wires they remind me of feet, robin-red-breasted feet cut off just above the ankle; flying, they remind me of feather-fingered hands flip-flopping themselves into the sky, palms down. For them the air is thick enough.

But I have one thing.

When I was young I felt the world two ways, by mouth and by that one impetuous finger (I cannot say between my legs) that would rise up in curiosity at any interesting texture or temperature. Now it seems not so inquisitive. But then, it has already tested cotton, wool, wood, paper, the wall, the floor, the reading stand and so forth. It has ventured—omnivorous, can one say?—into holes in the sheet. It has examined the interior of a velvet purse (silk-lined). It has pushed a toy car. It has entered a shoe. All this in its younger days.

There is, in my world, also— Well, it isn't really *my* world. As I said, mine would have to be a lot slushier. Anyway, I've got balance, rolling, flopping and the arching of the back. Balance I have never completely mastered. I suppose I should mention other small diversions such as defecating, urinating, the blinking of eyes, the wiggling of ears and watching TV.

And I've got drama, too. Down the hall at five o'clock or so comes Mrs. Number One all dressed up like a nurse. I think I must, at some time, have been bought outright, else why does she keep me on like this? She doesn't get paid anymore. Who would pay her? And what do I give in exchange for the emptying of bedpans or a lift into the bathroom, for food so considerately cut up so I can feed myself? Why, only what I can give. She likes it with brute force. "Rape, rape," she says, but not loud enough to attract attention outside of my little room.

I bounce her on the point of my one and only (or she makes me believe I do). Actually I couldn't rape an old glove. At the time I think I would not trade this one for any other protuberance, but afterward I think two legs are well worth one of these. However, the price is too high. If I had three of them it might be possible to come to some terms, but one, even as well-functioning as this . . . No sale!

Rape, rape, to me was Run, run.

That day (the day she locked the door and said, "If you ever tell . . ." But there wasn't anybody *to* tell. I think I was forgotten the moment I was born)—that day I thought I knew what running felt like. This was skimming over the earth, rampant, halfway to the ceiling with only the soles of the feet touching bottom. This was one foot, lightly, before the other, the swing of the leg underneath, the body riding smoothly on top of it all (amazing), the counterbalancing arms, back and forth, the toes giving a last push-off, the knee raised, bent, the foot circling upward, pivoting out, falling ahead to catch the ground, then pushing off again, and so on. Hundreds of takeoffs, and that's what this was, too, a hundred takeoffs until I flew into the air, but I came to rest again, flat upon the mattress.

I suppose she was grateful. One of us was.

She has been my nurse since God knows when, since before I knew what a calendar was or that time was anything but fresh sheets now and then. I must have been about ten, a backward, slobbery ten, when she came, squashing about on her nursing shoes. She squeaks when she turns. She bites into the floor, squashily sawtoothed, as if she felt as I do about the surfaces of things. Maybe she wanted me to have a better view of those aqueous soles of hers because the first thing she did was to have my mattress put upon the floor. I admit I gained in freedom and that my distances could then be measured. I learned that the wearing down at the heel was a long time.

But Mrs. Number One isn't the only person in my life. There is a Miss Number Two, oh, yes, and quite beautiful, too, Miss Spanish Eyes, Miss—I wonder if it would make any difference if Mrs. Number One were beautiful—Miss White Gloves (the white gloves just in case she might, by some mistake, touch me). She came to me fresh from racing cars, mountaintops, airplanes, at least it seemed so to me, but I see things from a floorish point of view. Everything may look like that from here.

What she brought first were the ABCs, then *Run, Tom, Run,* then *The Easy to Read Book of Far Away Places,* and all the way up to books-of-the-month and Shakespeare.

I think that Miss Number Two is, most probably, my sister. Not that there's ever been anything sisterly-brotherly between us, but I have a hundred clues. The most obvious, that she's always been around, one way or another, in a sneaky way even before she came to me with her books and that Nefertiti tip of her head. I remember a breezy kid not much younger than myself in a tree outside my window, blue jeans, red shirt, sticking out her tongue at me, and I happy that the gesture was one I could return. Now and again I remember a furious voice from some other part of the house screeching for her to "Get down, my God, get down." I remember an eye, brown, lustrous, like a little mouse nose waiting at the crack in the door, sometimes during my bath. I even remember the knob turning and the door opening to make that crack. Later a decision was made, out of a sense of obligation or out of resentment, and she, or someone else, decided and she came to me. I cannot say with happiness. I think I was happier before. What with five o'clock drama, everything seemed complete to me. No, it wasn't happiness and she knew it.

And yet I count on her for my salvation. If anyone is going to rescue me I know it will have to be bold Miss Number Two, and even though I first approached Mrs. Number One, it is Number Two I had in mind all the time. I was afraid. I was in such a cold sweat of hope that I didn't dare to go to Number Two and I didn't even mention to Number One what I really had in mind.

What a vision I had then . . . I still have. I see myself in a bright and revealing costume, all Harlequin colors and diamond shapes. I am in a stall with streamers, festoons and flags, American flags . . . no, flags of all nations. I belong to the world. Loudspeakers on the roof send out fanfares interspersed with Handel's "Fireworks" music and I, highlighted with a pinkish spotlight, perform upon my mattress such movements as I can perform (and many of these require the utmost skill and concentration). After the day's work, and I do think I can call it work, I see myself in a close and comfortable association with the rubber man, the fat lady, the human pincushion and the half man–half woman.

Though I have this grand vision in mind, and really even grander than this, for I see myself as a champion of champions— though I have this vision, I decided that I would ask only that Mrs. Number One should borrow a camera and should take a dozen pictures of me from various angles and in various poses. I thought I could not only use these in some way as an advertise- ment of myself, but also to get some real idea of myself since I had, so far, never seen myself in any way at all. It was from the pictures that I thought I could make my further decisions about my future. It's true that it's hard to be really self-evaluating but I thought I might judge well enough if I subtracted a certain percentage for too much self-love and another equal percentage for self-hate. The good thing about photographs would be that any initial shock I might have at my first real view of myself could be gotten over by getting used to the pictures. I felt I might get enlargements made and I would have Number One tack some along the walls and I promised myself I would make no decisions whatsoever for at least two weeks of living with them. Then I hoped to be able to look at myself with a truly cold eye.

She agreed. No arguments. Not a blink or shiver. No ambiguous glances, irresolute phrases or imponderable sighs. "O.K.," she said, and yet days passed and nothing happened. Finally I approached her firmly, my eyes my only weapon though they couldn't even stop her bustling about, swishing away nonexistent spots on the dresser front, picking little black threads off the rug. Yes, even at my five o'clock drama she is all business, that busy business of getting herself "raped" by me. Maybe she thinks it's part of her job, and yet now she keeps me all on her own as if I am some- thing she dressed up to amuse herself with, nothing but her back- room dildo.

Maybe this sex is *my* job.

But suppose I was inherited after my mother's death. Did I come with the house? A condition of its ownership? And I wonder if my mother, herself, could have paid for that first time. Or Miss Number Two. Did Mrs. Number One really say not to tell?

Impossible to know whose obligation this drama is, mine or Mrs. Number One's. No use wondering. I'll keep on doing my duty, or she hers, and I don't think that I, at least, will ever be able to find out. (But if I had anything more than just this one thing, then I could. One dactylic protuberance more to pit against the other in some way, one threat, one appeasement, one offering, one retreat, one gesture, one decline, one weapon other than this one, then I could find out who is the willing one and who the slave.)

However . . .

At this time I said to her that I believed she had no intention of going through with this photography business at all.

What I lacked, she told me then—"probably due to your environment . . . you can't be expected . . . so naïve . . . not like the rest of us . . ." and so on and on—what I lacked, it all came down to, was Good Taste, capital G, capital T, otherwise I would have known that a picture of myself would be an oh-so-gross violation of propriety and could certainly serve no good purpose either to others or to me, so, she said, she had decided from the beginning not to do it for my own good (as well as for everyone's) but I had been so forceful, so firm, she hadn't known how to argue with me . . . at that time, at least. She was, of course, terribly sorry about the whole thing. But, besides, what would the man who printed the pictures say? Chances were he wouldn't return them. Society sees to such things, she said. There are censors at work, even on photos, whether I knew it or not. (Can I, somehow, be lewd simply existing like this? Do I lie here on my sheets, pornographic every day? But hasn't everyone got his pornographic parts?)

At times like these, grasping at distracting details, I watch her nose point out her line of sight. Look ahead, it tells me, but life surely cannot be as earnest as most noses would have it be. Yet it is from this eager nose that I got the idea of asking to see my mother. I thought I might have more courage to speak out to someone I didn't know as well.

"Your mother," Number One said, "leads a comfortable life. She has surrounded herself with loveliness." (This I understand now much more than I did then, for it was to me that Mother willed many of her nice things. A handsome Louis XV table is now against my far wall, above it hangs a print of Madame Vigée-Lebrun and her daughter [all arms], upon it is a small statue of Hermes that used to be a salt and pepper holder.)

At this time, however, my room was more simply furnished. The mattress on the floor, the books lined up beside it, each with a little leather pull so I can grab it with my teeth—a slow process, finding one's page—book holder, chest of drawers, eating stand, not a single ornament unless you can call decorative a pinkish little creature Miss Number Two had brought me. She often brings things, all sorts, once a covered glass with three grasshoppers, once a white mouse, once a wounded bird. I suppose for my education, yet they give me great pleasure. This time she had been to the beach and had thought of me and brought back a jar of sea water with a starfish in it. (Even though there is no friendship or love between us, I am well aware that she constantly thinks of me. What must it be like to have me curled up at the back of your mind? Seeing everything as though through my eyes? Thinking that I have not walked upon this sand nor felt the edges of these grasses grate against my ankles? That I have not smelled the dried foam on the rocks? And never will? And so she brings these creatures to give me a realization that she herself has already. But I have always wondered, does she do it to torment me, as she may have brought the reading and the *Book of Far Away Places?* Does she do it for the torments of understanding so that I will come at last to really know?) The starfish gave me the most pleasure of all.

When I finally did convince Number One to arrange for a visit with my mother (during which Number One would be present, of course, since she feels herself a guardian of Good Taste—but I was ready to be the essence of propriety), this jar lay on the far corner of my eating stand. I would move my smallest pillow to the near edge of the stand and rest my chin there and watch the starfish feel its preposterously slow way along the glass. Note the suckers along the undersides of starfish fingers. You might say they are the starfish's tiny army. Commands move across them like a wind, a very slow wind, that is, over grass. Move, suck, release, and each starts a little after the one next to it.

This was not my first starfish, though the largest, and I have come to know them intimately. I have learned to love them in a way that I have not loved any other creature. I have thought: What if I had this army for my own? If this were my hand? My little suckers all along the palm? I have thought I might button a button, blow my nose, answer a telephone, turn out the light. I have thought I might feel my way across the floor, this star on the end of some long radius and ulna. I might risk the stairs, letting myself down, reaching lower and letting myself down again. I could run away and, even if it took all night, moving at a starfish pace, to get as far as the next house, I might find a hiding place to spend the day and set out farther the next night, each day finding a hovel or a thicket to rest in, never discovered, ever onward by silver moonlight.

Later, this same starfish was dried and it is still here upon my low shelf. I once felt it with my tongue and now I know the sea tastes of sauerkraut.

I insisted that I be dressed up for the interview in my best shirt and even a tie, though I never wore one; also, I never had the top button of my shirt buttoned, for you can imagine to what uses I have to put my neck. I wished, then, I had a jacket and a pair of real pants for the occasion. I thought they might be stretched out beyond me and a pair of shoes stuck into the pants legs. After all, so much of what we do is for show; why not, out of deference, do a little something extra? But Number One thought not. Still, she arranged a quilt very prettily up around my waist, made tea, brought out a box of pastries, combed my hair, wiped the sweat off my forehead. A pity I had no toes to tap, no knuckles to suck nervously, hardly anything to fidget until she came, but I chewed on my upper lip and posed myself as calmly and as aesthetically as I could manage, twisting slightly in a sort of reclining contrapposto.

And so Mother came in. She was wearing one of those basic blacks with a silver necklace and one could see at a glance that she was chock-full of cultivated charm. Sedate, nothing flashy or overdone. She crossed her legs and her little skirt snuggled up around her thighs, bonneting her stockinged knees, which leaned together like two nuns, a bit of white slip peeping out beside their cheeks. (Could she really be all this and pious, too?) I felt quite untidy beside them even in my best expression.

"Tea . . . a cake? . . . Disturbing news of Cuba . . . Yes, South America is so revolutionary . . . Cold for fall . . . an early frost . . . I was wondering . . ."

I remember best her feet (this is not unusual, considering my low position here upon my mattress) in little black pumps reflecting the squares of the window and reminding me of Number One's nose . . . something classical about them both, I guess. I would have liked to press my tongue across the shine of the shoes . . . well, yes, and the nose, too. (I still wonder what their flavors might have been, the nose certainly vanilla or apple, the shoes a red-winy taste soured by the sidewalks.)

(I do often wonder if *they* can appreciate flavors as I do, if *they* even know the real pleasures of eating. Certainly they have too many diversions and, though as babies they tested things as I test them, I am sure that, by now, they have forgotten the joys and understandings of tongue and lip.)

Mother, pressing her dactyls into lady fingers in a useless proliferation, had just said the view from my window was the best in the house and I had just said that I had been thinking about my future and would like to have her help, at least for some of the details, until I could get started on my own. "Future," Mother said, just at that moment glancing down, and then she saw it. She forgot the studied beauty of the classical smile, the corners of the mouth faintly Ionic but not yet Corinthian, and she forgot to watch out for those knees under that tight skirt of hers. Her eyes saw a wound . . . some horrible wound of the genitals, lustrous, blistered, purple. (And yet I suppose exposed genitals, pure and simple, healthily blooming and blushing, would be enough to cause her stunned and outraged look.) And my starfish was firm-bodied, beautifully turgid and a rosy, tan-pink color.

"What is that thing?" The way she said "thing," to flush it down the toilet was too good for it, though she would certainly want to dispose of it as quickly as one would dispose of a particularly hairy spider. . . . Still, nothing hairy here.

The starfish reclined (one might say) near the top of the jar, one finger hidden by the punctured lid, one stretched languidly sideways along the ridge where the glass curved, and three almost straight down. Infinitesimally, one of the lower fingers was edging upward. I don't believe Mother could have noticed this movement and certainly she couldn't have had time to examine or understand the waving suckers, yet gall touched her tongue and even her knees paled. I saw she saw the world in that jar, caught in that abyss, sour sea water all over it, and she, without wanting to, drinking its juices . . . or me. Was it me she thought she looked at? Opposites reflecting each other, he all digits and he of none? Whichever it was, I saw, in the shape of her lips, that the taste of death (or life) was on them and I held my breath.

That's the last I ever saw of her; isn't that strange? Those rejecting lips and then the shoes departing in uneven clicks, for though she was hardly half as old as Number One (but I must admit Number One keeps up her strength extraordinarily well, rinses it in, I suppose, with the henna of her hair, or sucks it from me with that avid other mouth. I do age fast)—for though she was hardly half, as I said—Mother, who refused ever after that to come into my room, died a year later. One could say that she faced her moment of truth with a starfish.

And so, after all, I have been forced into approaching Miss Number Two, whom, as I've already mentioned, I really felt to be my only salvation from the beginning, but instead of photographs (I had started with Number Two in exactly the same way I started with Number One in spite of the mention of a censor)—not understanding what I had in mind at all—instead of photographs, Number Two brought me a mirror, a rather large hand mirror, round and with a blue cast to the glass.

I was surprised to find that I had a handsome, rather noble head. No reactions, no expressions on any of the faces of those that had appeared before me had ever led me to believe that this might be. In fact, I was sure of the opposite and I had only hoped I might be passable. Also I found that I did resemble, to a surprising degree, Miss Number Two, and was, in my own masculine way, quite as attractive as she was, my hair the same mat black, my eyes mysterious, my cheeks with a mute, aristocratic pallor, my nose stark. I had a thick, muscular neck not exactly in keeping with my fine-featured face and, as she held the mirror farther from me, I saw a barrel-chested manatee-thing, certainly ichthyoid, with little wing shapes lumping under my clothes at hips and shoulders as though I could actually, as I've dreamed, swim into the air, and I saw the eyes of Number Two leaning to get the same view as I had of myself. I could see her thoughts reflecting my own! What a curious shape, and is it beautiful or ugly? Has it a meaning of its own? Is it a symbol of sloth or courage or of sex? Or is it a symbol at all?

"I had thought," I said to her eye as it floated languidly at the edge of the mirror—I could scarcely tell mine from hers, three haughty eyes there, moving slightly eastward about a foot under the watery surface, I would guess. I decided to speak to all three. "I had thought," I said, "that I might go on display." Two eyes remained immobile while the other contracted its lid a quarter of an inch. I could see I wasn't getting sympathy from any of them.

One of them closed for a moment, as though an eye could take a deep breath. Was it exasperated with me? Have you any concept at all, it seemed to be asking me, of what you really are? Does the fat lady, monstrous as she is, have anything to do with you? And the half man–half woman?

Ah, but *I* am certainly all male and perhaps nothing *but* male.

I see. Here, in other words, is the flying phallus at last, a truncated Hermes. Are you going on display for that? A little chicken Icarus (cut down, but winged, it is true) doing five o'clock drama in a different sort of back room?

But none of those eyes can know about that drama. They swim smugly in little back and forth motions, contracting their corners rhythmically in order to maintain their equilibrium. I see I have gone beyond the eyes. I'll tell them that fashions in freaks change; that, just as with sex; what was unacceptable last year is accepted this year. People always accept more as they become sophisticated, don't they? And isn't this equally desirable in freaks as in sex? Liberalize them, I say, and let me be one of those who struggle for this cause, this great opening out of understanding, this acceptance without censure. The presentation will make such a difference, too. We'll do it with finesse and delicacy. To start, I will take the name Désiré. And certainly with my so unforeseen personal beauty . . . But the eyes won't think so. I can see that. The two, led by the one most energetic and most opinionated, will agree with each other, and they will certainly feel that the mirror is too small a place for any arguments.

Let me approach them, instead, from the point of view of love. I might ask them: Shouldn't people be taught to love? People don't realize, I will say, how hard it is to love and that it must be practiced daily with some difficult exercise. And *I* might provide that exercise.

But I'm sure I won't be that hard to love. Everyone loves a winner and I'll be the freak of freaks. They'll come to think of me as beautiful. The details of my body might even be, eventually, exposed on TV. My life story might be written, and surely, if I did have such a life, there would be something to write about, such as how I first decided to join the carnival and the difficulties I had, in the beginning, in doing so; how they all doubted that I would be accepted by the public, for I was, after all, a new concept in freaks. I had, it was felt, carried freakishness to its ultimate degree. I was wholly and utterly the freak, whereas people were used to half freaks. It was felt I might be too startling. I might upset people. They might be more than just disgusted, but shaken to their very bones. But, at last, in some small circus side show, someone had had the courage to take me on. At first reactions were mixed. There were letters of protest: This was going too far . . . an insult to the public . . . poor taste that I should be where others could see me at all, let alone be on public view. I was even banned in a few cities, but of course this helped in the long run. Still, it was an uphill fight. Other freaks were jealous of my purity, my authenticity. No rubber, no makeup, no mutilation necessary. Yet I had my champions, including the circus owners who had invested in me, and also some freaks who were generously able to appreciate someone who was far beyond them. Still it will have taken me, let us suppose, about ten years to achieve any real acceptance. In any field one must certainly count on at least this much time, and I am not asking for a quick and easy success. And so, by then, people would have become used to me. Some would say I had a fishlike beauty, some that my movements were graceful and well adapted to my shape and to my needs. Some would argue that my achievements in rolling and flopping about had taken at least as much practice and concentration as would be needed by a concert pianist. Films would then be made to preserve my movements for posterity. Perhaps I might have had my body, by this time, tattooed with flowers and the faces of pretty girls. I would go on TV. The book on my life would be written, and in it, also, would be a description of how I came to be married and how I manage in my household with a little electric cart steered with my teeth, my children normal or almost normal (there is no need for my sort of mistake twice), and there would be something about my beautiful sister who helped me from the very beginning, at the first mention that I might be put on display.

"I had thought," I said, "that I might go on display. Yes, the carnival, the circus, no matter how small . . ."

But the fish eye had already given its answer.

"I suppose," said Number Two, "that you would like me to see that a proper suit is made, the beginnings of tights and a brocade . . . vest, shall we call it? Pink or blue? No, let's make it gold or silver with touches of red. I can sew it up myself out of silk and satin and, if you like, with little white wings to give the feeling of lightness to it all. Would you like them on the shoulder blades or buttocks?"

And she'll do it. I know she will and it will be better than I could possibly have conceived it myself, luminous as a peacock, gay as Santa Claus. I know Miss Number Two. Somehow, instinctively, she will touch the seed of my inner dream and make it grow into something greater than itself. Such work she will put into it! A month of hours. She'll hang it upon my wall and, with great joy, I'll dream of myself wearing it. I will grow old, leaning at my reading stand and dreaming. I know I will.

Then one day I will ask Mrs. Number One to put the suit on me. I will try (at least try, but she does have ways . . . warm water and such) to withhold all else until she does, and then I'll know if it really fits or only seems to.

Al

Sort of a plane crash in an uncharted region of the park.

We were flying fairly low over the mountains. We had come to the last ridge when there, before us, appeared this incredible valley. . . .

Suddenly the plane sputtered. (We knew we were low on gas but we had thought to make it over the mountains.

"I think I can bring her in." (John's last words.)

I was the only survivor.

A plane crash in a field of alfalfa, across the road from it the Annual Fall Festival of the Arts. An oasis on the edge of the parking area. One surivivor. He alone, Al, who has spent considerable time in France, Algeria and Mexico, his paintings without social relevance (or so the critics say) and best in the darker colors, not a musician at all yet seems to be one of us. He, a stranger, wandering in a land he doesn't remember and not one penny of our kind of money, creeping from behind our poster, across from it the once-a-year art experience for music lovers. Knowing him as I do now, he must have been wary then; view from our poster, ENTRANCE sign, vast parking lot, our red and

white tent, our EXIT on the far side, maybe the sound of a song—
a frightening situation under the circumstance, all the others dead
and Al having been unconscious for who knows how long? (the
scar from that time is still on his cheek), stumbling across the
road then and into our ticket booth.

"Hi."

I won't say he wasn't welcome. Even then we were wondering,
were we facing stultification? Already some of our rules had become rituals. Were we, we wondered, doomed to a partial relevance in our efforts to make music meaningful in our time? And
now Al, dropped to us from the skies (no taller than we are, no
wider and not even quite so graceful). Later he was to say:
"Maybe the artful gesture is lost forever."

We had a girl with us then as secretary, a long-haired change-
ling child, actually the daughter of a prince (there still are
princes), left out in the picnic area of a western state forest to be
found and brought up by an old couple in the upper middle
class (she still hasn't found this out for sure, but has always
suspected something of the sort), so when *I* asked Al to *my*
(extra) bedroom it was too late. (By that time he had already
pounded his head against the wall some so he seemed calm
and happy and rather well adjusted to life in our valley.) The
man from the *Daily* asked him how did he happen to become
interested in art? He said he came from a land of cultural giants
east of our outermost islands where the policemen were all poets.
That's significant in two ways.

About the artful gesture being lost, so many lost arts and also
soft, gray birds, etc., etc., etc. (The makers of toe shoes will have
to go when the last toe dancer dies.)

However, right then, there was Al, mumbling to us in French,
German and Spanish. We gave him two tickets to our early-
evening concert even though he couldn't pay except in what
looked like pesos. Second row, left side. (Right from the beginning there was something in him I couldn't resist.) We saw him

144

craning his neck there, somehow already with our long-haired girl beside him. She's five hundred years old though she doesn't look a day over sixteen and plays the virginal like an angel. Did her undergraduate work at the University of Utah (around 1776, I would say). If she crossed the Alleghenies *now* she'd crumble into her real age and die, so later on I tried to get them to take a trip to the Ann Arbor Film Festival together, but naturally she had something else to do. Miss Haertzler.

As our plane came sputtering down I saw the tents below, a village of nomads, God knows how far from the nearest outpost of civilization. They had, no doubt, lived like this for thousands of years.

These thoughts went rapidly through my mind in the moments before we crashed and then I lost consciousness.

"COME, COME YE SONS OF ART." That's what our poster across the street says, quotes, that is. Really very nice in Day-Glo colors. "COME, COME AWAY . . ." etc., on to "TO CELEBRATE, TO CELEBRATE THIS TRIUMPHANT DAY," which meant to me, in some symbolic way even at that time, the day Al came out from behind it and stumbled across the road to our booth, as they say, "a leading force, from then on, among the new objectivists and continues to play a major role among them up to the present time" (which was a few years ago). Obtained his bachelor's degree in design at the University of Michigan with further study at the Atelier Chaumière in Paris. He always says, "Form speaks." I can say I knew him pretty well at that time. I know he welcomes criticism but not too early in the morning. Ralph had said (he was on the staff of the Annual Fall Festival), "Maybe artistic standards are no longer relevant." (We were wondering at the time how to get the immediacy of the war into our concerts more meaningfully than the "1812 Overture." Also something of the changing race relations.) Al answered, but just then a jet came by or some big oil truck and I missed the key word. That leaves me still not understanding what he meant. The next morning the same thing happened and it may have been more or less the answer to everything.

By then we had absorbed the major San Francisco influences. These have remained with us in some form or other up to the present time. Al changed the art exhibit we had in the vestibule to his kind of art as soon as Miss Haertzler went to bed with him. We had a complete new selection of paintings by Friday afternoon, all hung in time for the early performance (Ralph hung them) and by then, or at least by Saturday night, I knew I was, at last, really in love for the first time in my life.

When I came to, I found we had crashed in a cultivated field planted with some sort of weedlike bush entirely unfamiliar to me. I quickly ascertained that my three companions were beyond my help, then extricated myself from the wreckage and walked to the edge of the field. I found myself standing beneath a giant stele where strange symbols swirled in brilliant, jewellike colors. Weak and dazed though I was, I felt a surge of delight. Surely, I thought, the people who made this cannot be entirely uncivilized.

Miss Haertzler took her turn on stage like the rest of us. She was the sort who would have cut off her right breast the better to bow the violin, but, happily, she played the harpsichord. Perhaps Al wouldn't have minded, anyway. Strange man. From some entirely different land and I could never quite figure out where. Certainly he wouldn't have minded. She played only the very old and the very new, whereas *I* had suddenly discovered Beethoven (over again) and I talked about Romanticism during our staff meetings. Al said, "In some ways a return to Romanticism is like a return to the human figure." I believe he approved of the idea.

He spent the first night, Tuesday night, that was, the twenty-second, in our red and white tent under the bleachers at the back. A touch of hay fever woke him early.

By Wednesday Ralph and I had already spent two afternoons calculating our losses due to the rain, and I longed for a new experience of some sort that would lift me out of the endless problems of the Annual Fall Festival of the Arts. I returned dutifully, however, to the area early the next day to continue my calculations in the quiet of the morning and found him there.

"Me, Al. You?" Pointing finger.

"Ha, ha." (I *must* get rid of my nervous laugh!)

I wanted to redefine my purposes not only for his sake, but for my own.

I wanted to find out just what role the audience should play.

I wanted to figure out, as I mentioned before, how we could best incorporate aspects of the war and the changing race relations into our concerts.

I wondered how to present musical experiences in order to enrich the lives of others in a meaningful way, how to engage, in other words, their total beings. I wanted to expand their musical horizons.

"I've thought about these things all year," I said, "ever since I knew I would be a director of the Annual Fall Festival. I also want to mention the fact," I said, "that there's a group from the college who would like to disrupt the unity of our performances (having other aims and interests) but," I told him, "the audience has risen to the occasion, at least by last night, when we had not only good weather, but money and an enthusiastic reception."

"I have recognized," he replied, "here in this valley, a fully realized civilization with a past history, a rich present, and a future all its own, and I have understood, even in my short time here, the vast immigration to urban areas that must have taken place and that must be continuing into the present time."

How could I help but fall in love with him? He may have

spent the second night in Miss Haertzler's bed (if my conjectures are correct) but, I must say, it was with me he had all his discussions.

I awoke the next morning extremely hungry, with a bad headache and with sniffles and no handkerchief, yet somehow, in spite of this, in fairly good spirits though I did long for a good hot cup of almost anything. Little did I realize then, or I might not have felt so energetic, the hardships I was to encounter here in this strange, elusive, never-never land. Even just getting something to eat was to prove difficult.

Somewhat later that day I asked him out to lunch and I wish I could describe his expression eating his first grilled cheese and bacon, sipping his first clam chowder. . . .

Ralph, I tell you, this really happened and just as if we haven't *all* crash-landed here in some sort of (figurative) unknown alfalfa field. As if we weren't *all* penniless or about to be, waiting for you to ask us out to lunch. Three of our friends are dead and already there are several misunderstandings. You may even be in love with me for all I know, though that may have been before I had gotten to be your boss in the Annual Fall Festival.

That afternoon I gave Al a job, Ralph, cleaning up candy wrappers and crumpled programs with a nail on a stick, and I invited him to our after-performance party for the audience. Paid him five dollars in advance. That's how much in love I was, so there's no sense in you coming over anymore. Besides, I'm tired of people who play instruments by blowing.

I found the natives to be a grave race, sometimes inattentive, but friendly and smiling, even though more or less continuously concerned about the war. The younger ones frequently live communally with a charming innocence, by threes or fours or even up to sixes or eights in quite comfortable apartments, sometimes forming their own family groups from a few chosen

*friends, and, in their art, having a strange return to the very
old or the primitive along with their logical and very right
interest in the new, though some liked Beethoven.*

We had invited the audience to our party after the performance.
The audience was surprised and pleased. It felt privileged. It
watched us now with an entirely different point of view and it
wondered at its own transformation while I wondered why I
hadn't thought of doing this before and said so to Al as the
audience gasped, grinned, clapped, fidgeted and tried to see into
the wings.

We had, during that same performance, asked the audience
to come forward, even to dance if it was so inclined. We had discussed this thoroughly beforehand in our staff meetings. It wasn't
as though it was not a completely planned thing, and we had
thought some Vivaldi would be a good way to start them off.
Al had said, "Certainly something new must happen every day."
Afterward I said to the audience, "Let me introduce Al, who has
just arrived by an unfortunate plane crash from a far-off land,
a leading force among the new objectivists, but penniless at the
moment, sleeping out under our bleachers. . . ." However, that
very night I heard that Miss Haertzler and Al either went for a
walk after our party up to the gazebo on the hill or they went
rowing on the lake, and I heard someone say, though not neces-
sarily referring to them, "Those are two thin young people in the
woods and they're quite conscious that they don't have clothes
on and that they're very free spirits." And someone said, "She
has a rather interesting brassiere," though that was at a different
time, and also, "I wonder if he's a faggot because of the two
fingers coming down so elegantly."

*I found it hard to adjust to some of the customs of this hardy
and lively people. This beautiful, slim young girl invited me to
her guest room on my second night there and then entered as
I lay in bed, dropping her simple, brightly colored shift at her*

feet. Underneath she wore only the tiniest bit of pink lace, and while I was wondering, was she, perhaps, the king's daughter or the chief's mistress? what dangers would I be opening myself up to? and thinking besides that this was my first night in a really comfortable bed after a very enervating two days, also my first night with a full stomach and would I be able to? she moved, not toward me, but to the harpsichord. . . .

I had much to learn.

Mornings, sometimes as early as nine-thirty, Al could be found painting in purples, browns, grays and blacks in the vestibule area at the front of our tent. The afternoons many of us, Al included, frequently spent lounging on the grass outside the tent (on those days when it didn't rain), candidly confessing the ages of and the natures of our very first sexual experiences and discussing other indiscretions, with the sounds of the various rehearsals as our background music. (Miss Haertzler's first sexual experience, from what I've been told, may have actually taken place fairly recently and in our own little red ticket booth.) Thinking back to those evening concerts I can still see Al, as though it were yesterday, in his little corner backstage scribbling on his manifesto of the new art:

"Why should painting remain shackled by outmoded laws? Let us proclaim, here and at once, a new world for art where each work is judged by its own internal structures, by the manifestations of its own being, by its self-established decrees, by its self-generated commands.

"Let us proclaim the universal properties of the thing itself without the intermediary of fashion.

"Let us proclaim the fragment, the syllable, the single note (or sound) as the supreme elements out of which everything else flows. . . ."

And so forth.

(Let us also proclaim what a friend [Tom Disch] has said: "I don't understand people who have a feeling of comfortableness about art. There's a kind of art that they feel comfortable seeing and will go and see that kind of thing again and again. I get very bored with known sensations. . . .")

But, even as Al worked, seemingly so contented, and even as he welcomed color TV, the discovery of DNA and the synthesizing of an enzyme, he had his doubts and fears just like anyone else.

Those mountains that caught the rays of the setting sun and burned so red in the evenings! That breathtaking view! How many hours did I spend gazing at them when I should have been writing on my manifesto, aching with their beauty and yet wondering whether I would ever succeed in crossing them? How many times did my conversation at that time contain hidden references to bearers and guides? Once I learned of a trail that I might follow by myself if I could get someone to furnish me with a map. It was said to be negotiable only through the summer to the middle of October and to be too steep for mule or motorcycle. Later on I became acquainted with a middle-aged homosexual flute player named Ralph, who was willing to answer all my questions quite candidly. We became good friends and, as I got to know him better, I was astounded at the sophistication of his views on the nature of the universe. He was a gentle, harmless person, tall and tanned from a sun lamp. Perhaps I should mention that he never made any sexual advances to me, that I was aware of at any rate.

"After the meeting between Ralph A. and Al W.," the critics write, "Ralph A.'s work underwent an astonishing change. Obviously he was impressed by the similarities between art and music and he attempted to interpret in musical terms those portions of Al W.'s manifesto that would lend themselves to this transposition. His 'Three Short Pieces for Flute, Oboe and Prepared Piano' is, perhaps, the finest example of his work of this period."

By then Al had lent his name to our town's most prestigious art gallery. We had quoted him often in our programs. I had discussed with him the use of public or private funds for art. I had also discussed, needless to say, the problem of legalized abortion and whether the state should give aid to parochial schools. Also the new high-yield rice. I mentioned our peace groups including our Women's March for Peace. I also tried to tell him Miss Haertzler's real age and I said that, in spite of her looks, it would be very unlikely that she could ever have any children, whereas I, though not particularly young anymore, could at least do that, I'm (fairly) sure.

And then, all too soon, came the day of the dismantling of the Annual Fall Festival tent and the painting over of our billboard, which Al did (in grays, browns, purples and blacks), making it into an ad for the most prestigious art gallery, and I, I was no longer a director of anything at all. The audience, which had grown fat and satiated on our sounds, now walked in town as separate entities . . . factions . . . fragments . . . will-o'-the-wisp . . . meaningless individuals with their separate reactions. Al walked with them, wearing his same old oddly cut clothes as unself-consciously as ever, and, as ever, with them but not of them. He had worked for us until the very last moment, but now I had no more jobs to give. He couldn't find any other work and, while the critics and many others, too, liked his paintings, no one wanted to buy them. They were fairly expensive and the colors were too somber. I helped him look into getting a grant, but in the end it went to a younger man (which I should have anticipated). I gave him, at about that time, all my cans of corned beef hash even though I knew he still spent some time in Miss Haertzler's guest room, though, by then, a commune (consisting of six young people of both sexes in a three-room apartment) had accepted him as one of them. (I wonder sometimes that he never asked Miss Haertzler to marry him, but he may have been unfamiliar with marriage as we know it. We never discussed it that I remember and not too many people in his circle of friends were actually married to each other.)

Ralph had established himself as the local college musical figure, musician in residence really, and began to walk with a stoop and a slight limp and to have a funny way of clearing his throat every third or fourth word. I asked him to look into a similar job for Al, but they already had an artist in residence, a man in his sixties said to have a fairly original eye and to be profoundly concerned with the disaffection of the young, so they couldn't do a thing for Al for at least a year, they said, aside from having him give a lecture or two, but even that wouldn't be possible until the second semester.

Those days I frequently saw Al riding around on a borrowed motor scooter (sometimes not even waving), Miss Haertzler on the back with her skirts pulled up. He still painted. The critics have referred to this time in his life as one of hardship and self-denial while trying to get established.

Meanwhile it grew colder.

Miss Haertzler bought him a shearling lamb jacket. Also one for herself. I should have suspected something then, but I knew it was the wrong time of year for a climb. There was already a little bit of snow on the top of the highest of our mountains and the weatherman had forecast a storm front on the way that was to be there by that night or the next afternoon. We all thought it was too early for a blizzard.

I was to find Miss (Vivienne) Haertzler an excellent traveling companion. Actually a better climber than I was myself in many ways and yet, for all that vigor, preserving an essential femininity. Like many others of her race, she had small hands and feet and a fair-skinned look of transparency, and yet an endurance that matched my own. But I did notice about her that day an extraordinary anxiety that wasn't in keeping with her nature at all (nor of the natives in general). I didn't give a second thought, however, to any of the unlikely rumors I had heard, but I assumed it was due to the impending storm that we hoped would hide all traces of our ascent.

A half day later a good-sized group of our more creative people were going after one of the most exciting minds in the arts with bloodhounds. A good thing for Miss Haertzler, too, since the two of them never even got halfway. I saw them back in town a few days afterward, still looking frostbitten, and it wasn't long after that that I had a very pleasant discussion with Al. I had asked him out to our town's finest continental restaurant. We talked, among other things, about alienation in our society, population control, impending world famine and other things of international concern including the anxiety prevalent among our people of impending atomic doom. In passing I mentioned a psychologist I had once gone to for certain anxieties of my own of a more private nature. Soon after that I heard that Al was in therapy himself and had learned to accept his perennial urge to cross the mountains and, as the psychologist put it, "leave our happy valley in his efforts to escape from something in himself." It would be a significant moment in both modern painting and modern music (and perhaps in literature, too) when Al would finally be content to remain in his new-found artistic milieu. I can't help but feel that the real beginning of Al's participation (sponsored) within our culture as a whole was right here on my couch in front of the fireplace with a cup of hot coffee and a promise of financial assistance from two of our better-known art patrons. It was right here that he began living out some sort of universal human drama of life and death in keeping with his special talents.

Methapyrilene Hydrochloride
Sometimes Helps

I am not sick. I have been healed of all my various ills by Dr.
Alexander D. Ostrander, my doctor for the last ten years. I am
now, he says, of these various ills cured. I believe he's written
it officially on some hospital form or other: Mrs. Room 318 will
be considered, that is until some new morbidity, completely
recovered.

However, I cannot think of myself as, though well, exactly
normal. In my case wellness is relative. Cured is simply the ab-
sence of the initial putrefying elements. But Dr. Ostrander has
convinced me that I can consider myself at least 20 percent
normal in every respect. I like that and I keep thinking about
my normal aspects and how they are bridges to reality and factors
enabling me, still, to study the world as it is. Thank God, that is,
for one arm and one leg as yet completely untouched by any
aspect of medical science.

But let me tell you my exact situation as of now. My body,
my actual body (due to circumstances entirely native to my
twentieth-century environment), is, as I've mentioned, considered
by physicians to be approximately 20 percent normal. I owe, as
they say, my life to the machine that beats my heart. I owe my
bright eyes and my clear complexion to my twice-daily hand-held

bowel irrigation accomplished through a permanent hole in the right lower abdominal quadrant. The functioning of my right leg and right side is, on the other hand, left somewhat impaired by the removal of a tumor in the lower thoracic region of the spinal cord.

My heart-beating box, by the way, goes neither click-click nor tick-tock. It does its work more silently than the heart itself, and Dr. Ostrander says that in spite of cold, heat, exercise and passions, it should continue at an even and restrained eighty beats per minute. So, I feel, the essential *I* remains in spite of it all. (It's rumored that a new model will soon be out enabling the heart to beat at more comfortably adjustable rates of from seventy to eighty-five bpm.)

There are those who keep asking me why I wear this little heart-beating box against my left side and why I wear my, as we could call it, bladder strapped to my inner thigh. They wonder, even, at the unfeminine loss of hair and perhaps, at least I wouldn't be surprised, they think: What is that strange, illusive, yet not unsweet smell?

Sometimes they wonder, have I caused all this to be done to myself, in some strange way, on purpose? They ask me, do I say to myself that I, at least, have brought this to myself while their asymmetricalities are inborn? Certainly they notice that they are not "their own" in the sense that I am "mine."

Listening, sitting in my own special version of the lotus position, I think how to overcome inertia in favor of some organic and perpetual peristalsis of the brain. Oh, not for myself. It's for others (mankind) that I make this study. (I am, by the way, only interested in impossibilities. People make their livings every day from the possible, while I, even in my psychological being, am not so particularly possible anymore.)

Listening, sitting in my own special version, I think that Dr. Ostrander may enter at any moment bringing new cures. He will prescribe three-colored capsules when he sees how I've cluttered my room with remote-controlled devices of alarm. (I'm here alone at night.)

He can, at any time, turn off the essential machine of my beating being. (I may be too old to have any more children now, anyway, as he often tells me.)

"Madam, cease this mad prancing after life," he will certainly say. "The eternal feminine is in some entirely other direction, as you should know by now."

"Really, doctor, if you would take your forefinger off my breast I think I could listen to you more profitably."

"My dear lady, you will find that the depths of womanhood (note I don't say ladyhood) lie in the inner soul rather than the outer body. We know you other-sexed creatures, though, by your haircut and your pointed toes (though this is changing) rather than by any apparent vaginal orifice or by any perceptible emanations from the soul."

"Dr. Ostrander, dear, if you would remove your thumb from the probing of the uterus, I would not find my mind in this post-philosophical state, and the ratios of comprehension to number of words per five-minute period would appreciably rise to levels we would all realize immediately. Besides, the lotus position is, under these circumstances, even more uncomfortable than it is necessary for it to become in one full hour of spiritual contemplation."

"Black lace underwear makes all the difference, too, but, by the way, I do not think the accouterments you find yourself compelled to wear in your desperate clinging to existence, such as your essential left-sided machine and the external bladder, I do not find them contributing to your femininity in the least. Perhaps you are of an age and condition when you should give up sex altogether."

"Doctor, do you feel I must do so immediately?"

"Let me tell you that, as you well know, I am the father of a motherless and nubile daughter and I'm seeing to it that she grows up with, hopefully, all her primary and secondary sexual characteristics intact. Already her little breasts tickle me when I kiss her good night."

"Move a trifle to the left, please, and gently, Dr. O. You've removed already, I'm afraid, the Fallopian tubes, in spite (or because) of the difficulties and awkwardness of this position. Perhaps they caught on your thumbnail. (If you weren't so careless I might, even at this late date, have heartbeats from my very own electrical charges.)"

And so here we are again. What I mean is, we do return to the present environment, as usual. No matter what desperate, dreadful or, on the other hand, marvelous experiences we've been through, we seem always to return eventually to the present situation. The present, we might say, though it seems sometimes so remote, is always with us. In some ways, I mean after deaths and disasters, for instance, this is a fortunate thing, this coming back to the ever present present.

However (and because of this), now, again, one could repeat: Dr. Alexander Ostrander may enter at any moment bringing new cures, bringing three-colored capsules when he sees how I've changed my room because I really am alone here every night. Booby traps are all around. I even have advanced warning of the dear doctor's approach. Bells ring. Lights tell me his feet are eighteen inches from the door and wearing rubbers. He's only vaguely aware that I've prepared myself for him already. Before he can snatch the door open, here I am: the odalisque! Most of me that shows is still here. I have all my surfaces intact except for thin red lines here and there, ventral and dorsal.

But let me say that my warning system has already guessed that Dr. Ostrander is about to remove the spleen and a small portion of one kidney. Anything for a better disposition, he says, but I'm getting the feeling I should take my heartbeat box and run. My warning system is certainly inadequate except to notify, unless, in some way, I can transfer from flashing lights to machine guns. But what is the motivation for all these removals? What obsession compels him, in this way, to mutilate what he most loves? for certainly a doctor should love a body. But maybe they're loving subcutaneously to the smooth esophagus, the round red kidneys, the worming bowels. Their love is deeper and more subtle than I had thought. Oh, dear Dr. O., have I misjudged you all this time?

Actually Dr. Ostrander's daughter has often visited me, too, all nubile and her breasts expanding by, I would estimate, approximately one-quarter of an inch each week.

(Oh, Mrs. Room 318, how glad I am that you once, long ago, had children of your own.)

"There are inside changes as well as these outside changes so I'm taking the liberty, my dear, of describing to you some essentials of the menstrual cycle, for, after all, you're a motherless girl of twelve and who's to tell you these things if not I, one of your father's oldest and certainly best-loved patients? Now don't be alarmed if there's blood. It's all perfectly natural though it is mysterious. But let me quote from one of the latest national magazines: Many women experience premenstrual tension and this may show itself in irritability, nervousness, depression, fatigue, sensitivity. Newspapers say that at this time we're prone to auto accidents. Mensa-tex at two dollars a bottle may be helpful for cramps. Also these mild exercises which I now demonstrate in spite of my condition."

So here we are and she's gone again (it seems the present is usually empty) and here I am listening and sitting and what, I'm asking myself, as usual, can I as *I* give to the world-in-general? taking for granted that all of us have something to give, that is.

I don't believe, actually, that an enumeration of my minute and excruciating feelings as I underwent my various operations could be of a really unique service even if I were the only person to experience them all with the handsome, though no longer young, Dr. Alexander D. Ostrander at my side. My message, I feel, lies perhaps in my *joie de vivre,* in my hasty forward steps into "life itself," my electrical presence, my . . . for I'm certainly, even lying here all odalisque, *engagé* in a way many more active people can never be.

But, on the other hand, an enumeration does serve some purpose and I'm thinking that perhaps not many people are familiar with a bowel irrigation done by hand at eight-thirty every morning and evening. (This is done when the lower section of the rectum has been removed for one reason or another, usually cancer.) I have this little other ass hole. I insert there (left lower abdominal quadrant) an enema nozzle. (I keep this little hole covered, always, with a clean gauze in case of leakage.) I proceed as in all enemas, then remove the nozzle and hold against my side a little horned-moon-shaped pan. Afterward one must rinse the contents down into the toilet. It's best not to eat onions or cucumbers or beans.

Dr. Alexander Ostrander taught me how to do it and he was very patient. "A thing like this," he says, "is all right for men, but my God, woman, what do you take yourself for!"

Maybe Another Long
March Across China
80,000 Strong

Women!

Take me to your leader!

You seem to be on your way to some distant mountain strong-hold where you will retreat from all males except perhaps one or two. There seems to be thousands of you trudging along here, if my estimate is correct, while only a fraction of you will reach your destination. The biggest and strongest women are out in front. The grandmothers are toward the back, helped by their teen-age granddaughters. You stumble. Your knees are bleeding. Your toes are stubbed. You have scraped your elbows, sprained your ankles, yet still you keep on, gathering wild greens as you go, cooking one-pot meals over tiny fires, your smaller children piggyback or in slings, or you lean forward under huge knapsacks. Leading you, a chubby older lady of sixty-five or so who looks a little like George Washington. Look out! That rock is falling, pushed by some men, no doubt, who are up on the ridge. It almost lands on the George Washington lady, whose name is Betty though they call her Big Ma. She doesn't flinch.

Women! Oh, Women!

I want to go where you're going.

I want to join you even if it means leaving my son.

I want to sleep by the rushing streams where you'll be sleeping. I want to cut saplings and cover them with leaves and camp there. I want to climb all day long in the heat or the cold, I don't care which, and I want to dodge behind rocks when the men take pot shots. I want to see avalanches, forest fires. I want to see great rivers that have to be crossed, and mountain ranges. I want to face starvation.

Some of you are dying every day from one cause or another, but I want to go with you, anyway, singing your songs.

Big Ma is smiling. Whoever leads on to the end maybe will be president someday, maybe sit on the supreme court, maybe be governor of New York or head of General Motors, dean of Harvard Law School.

Fill out forms. Registration signed by Liz, Pat and Fran. "Brown eyes, small breasts, hair so short it won't be any trouble, bedroll, harmonica, big, floppy hat, and: "What was your relationship with your mother?" I contribute a couple of thousand dollars of my husband's money from our joint account (I hope he doesn't notice) and I have my own bag of granola.

My group: Bea, Kate, Marge, Mavis, Billie, Sandy, Sal . . .

Get out of my way, all you untried and untempered young girls. It's old Sandy, ugly Isabelle, tough little Shirl, red-faced Amy, gravel-throated Jo for me.

Just then a tall, dark man comes up asking to be made an honorary woman just for this year. He says he'll pay his own way and more, and eat what we do, dress like us. "I'll gather mushrooms." (He knows how.) "I'll give up ties and jockstraps if that's necessary. I'll enroll my sister if she wants to come, but my daughter belongs to one of my wives. I had three and I loved them each in turn, but unforeseen things happened every day. Now I hardly know them. Two left me and I left one. Even so, I joined the

Society of Friends of Women. Our branch made a study of the effect of hormones on energy levels but we didn't dare tell what we found out about testosterone. Also I have already apologized to my mother. 'Mother,' I said, 'forgive me for my diapers and all the various stages of my growing up and especially for that year I was thirteen.' "

"Oh," the tall, dark man says, "oh, to be establishing a whole new sense of self-worth! To be about to become! And I could wish I were small," he says, "and finer-featured. Once I met a famous Japanese female impersonator. Compared to me, he was a very delicate man.

"But the real reason I'm here," he says, "is that I have a new concept of leadership and I want to train women in ten lessons or less with little leadership situations that are likely to arise in everyday life. Some can even be practiced in the home on a husband and children."

"Well, all right then. Let him come along for now."

One hundred virgins march in his group, not one of them over eighteen.

Rivers are changing their courses where our feet have worn ruts that they find easier to take than their own riverbeds. (That's a good sign.) A few flakes of snow come down and twilight comes earlier by a minute and a half every day.

The higher we climb the older I get.

I have wrinkles at the corners of my eyes. My frown is permanent. I squint to watch the booted, belted girls silhouetted by the sunrise. They tramp back and forth on guard duty, while the older women, still wrapped in their blankets, cook eggs on stones. Men have been seen in the hills across the way from us. Nobody knows how many. Girls cock their crossbows and let fly a few warning darts, some tipped with sleeping potions made from herbs known only to women, and Marge, handsome as a black-eyed boy, makes up a new song.

That night we eat wild goat.

Next morning I catch sight of two transvestites in mini-skirts stumbling up the banks below us on high-heeled sandals. What can they be up to? (Also who knows how many blue-jeaned transvestites we already have hiding among us?) I'm not one to say what should or shouldn't be, and I welcome diversity and eclecticism of all kinds, so I yell: "Halloo."

Jimmy, the first one up to my ledge, has a beautiful blo.d Afro. I wonder if it's real.

"Howdy, partner."

Of course, they want to join us. Everybody does. But where do you draw the line? I tell them: "I can make you an honorary Negro, but not an honorary woman at this time," but they don't believe me. In spite of the leadership classes, I still haven't the aura of authority. What's needed is a big bass voice.

Jimmy really is quite beautiful in his own way.

"I've changed my mind," I say. "I *will* make you an honorary woman, if you aren't already one, and you can even be part of my group, but you'll have to go through the ceremony."

George, the second transvestite, finally reaches our ledge. He has a carrot-colored Afro that I'm pretty sure is real. He crosses his legs so his miniskirt won't show too much.

"I like your shoes."

Tall, dark man in the distance. Can it be me he's looking at?

Women, you're sleeping huddled together against the cold in groups of four or five. Your toes are freezing. You're remembering your electric blankets and the warm bodies of your husbands and lovers. You're thinking of times when you turned up thermostats. You're remembering cats that slept on your feet. In the night your mothers die, but this was not unexpected. "Why," you are asking, "did I tell her to come along with us? Surely I knew how hard it would be." You're beginning to wonder, is this the way? You're asking yourselves, "Do you really think things will get better just because you're doing something about it?" But lie down now, with your backs to the wind, and try not to think. One of these days it'll be: Greetings from Woman's Land! Like: Dear Tom. We are feasting like gods and only the men are cooks. We have banana trees. We love each other. Even the fat and the old go naked. What a relief! We do not worry about the shapes of our breasts. We plant and harvest. We swim. While our youngest daughters play in the surf, our oldest daughters photograph the sunsets. If we want to, we meditate or dance. Boys who are born here will be entirely new kinds of men. In the meantime, many of us have become great thinkers and presidents of our own organizations.

Marge lays out the tarot. "There's a king of cups in your past and a knight of wands in your future," she says, but I don't believe in cards.

I take George and Jimmy aside to explain to them about being a woman. "Taking a shower during those days of the month is even more necessary than at other times," I say, and, "Being a woman is a commitment of your whole being, not an off and on thing to be taken lightly. Burn your bras if you like," I say, "but there's a lot more to it than that, and where are the women doctors, lawyers, biochemists, philologists coming from, if not from you?" I ask. "But I'm not the high priestess. I only said that to make an impression. You'll have to go to Big Ma for the last and the best. I hope you make it."

My health is failing. If anyone falls in love with me now I'll be too tired for any sexual reciprocation. My nose runs. That will detract from my kisses. At night, after a long climb, my legs twitch. I have pimples on my eyelids. As of this morning, my voice is hoarse. And still, one falls in love in any condition and any situation. I watch those two young men and sense, from behind a bush, eyes on me. I can't see him but I know he's there.

"Pardon me, madam, but you seem to have dropped your cowboy hat."

Close up, I see Tall and Dark is almost as old as I am, but perhaps he's a man of no background in spite of his good looks.

"Sir, the baby on my back is not my own. I'm just doing this for a friend who needs help. Its name is Jane but I suspect it's a boy. Life is like this march, don't you think? On and on and ever upward. Cold these last few days. But sometimes the ontology of this whole thing escapes me. Oh, carry me off to some warm climate. Kiss away my tears. Am I giving up when I say that?"

But I have heard the dark man speaking Spanish in a whisper and I wonder if we are to be betrayed. His love may be one more attack. Pick out the old and sick, the stragglers, his penis as his weapon. In a way, he loves what he hates. I wonder what the psychology of that is. Once I overheard a group of young men say they'd like to get some hostile old lady they knew and rape her two or three times apiece. That would teach her a lesson. What did they mean by that? Would she be wise and gentle in the morning or dead from it, a final realization in her rolled-back eyes?

This night is darker than all the rest. My chastity is astonishing at a time like this. Whatever Tall and Dark wants to teach me now, I won't learn it. He said, "I like to see some spirit in my women. I like spunk and the fire in the eye. A woman like that is worth having," but that was before I kicked him in the groin. Well, I do know men have feelings, too, sometimes; longings, hopes and fears. They have their sad and pensive times of wonderment and awe, passions, moments of quiet withdrawal, sometimes covering up their mistakes with savoir-faire or a certain finesse.

"I love you," he said, but I knew he hardly knew me.

"Nowadays we don't want that kind of love."

"I've watched you from afar. I carved your name on the side of the cliff. Blow your nose. Take off your glasses and let me kiss you just once." But I wasn't sure how I felt so I gave him another kick.

As I said, this was our darkest night and I caught myself with a tear in my eye in spite of myself, but it was really not a feasible time for passions of any sort. Also I wanted to test him, so I said I would go down into the valley and get my first man so I could wear a little gold mark like some of the younger ones do. (Those men were only sheep ranchers, anyway.) Drying my tears, I said, "Give me five or six stout-hearted women and I'll find out what's going on over there on the opposite ridge." Pat, Kim, Liz, Lib, Fran, Bea, Barb, then, led by me, sneaking down, one behind the other, and maybe never coming back, and perhaps secretly followed by Tall and Dark, if he really loves me.

All I've got with me now is five feet of clothesline, a sandwich and an apple. All I've got with me is a lead dildo on a leather thong, one or two tricks I learned from my mother, my sharp eyes and the memory of past slights. I hope they stand me in good stead.

Women! (I say, Women! Like men say, Men!) Women! You are wild and free, shaking your shaggy manes, eyes like stormy skies, bouncing your breasts, sure-footed, savage, silent on the mountains, your whispered battle cries tentatively spoken in the dark, but about to ring out the sunlight. I want to be like you, thumbs in my belt loops, the baby girl on my back, one from those that were left out in the cold to die, for we have taken all the unwanted girls along with us to grow up wild and free, riding their ponies along the beaches of Woman's Land in the lee of what used to be known as Sleeping Woman mountain but now we call Sleeping Man. Still, it's true. All mountains look like women, all women look like mountains. They can't help it. I don't know if that's good or bad, but oh, I hope that that baby Jane is really one of those unwanted little girls, born into some family with seven or eight football-playing brothers. But I looked before I left and she's a boy after all. Somebody's unwanted little boy all dressed in pink. I think I understand him. I *know* I do. He must have had six older sisters, poor thing. I'll keep him and name him John.

Women! You've always tried to avoid all-out war (it's to your credit), though you've never avoided skirmishes and have even hoped for moral confrontations and tests of. skills, but you will not put up with any more discussions. You are quoting, now, from outstanding women of bygone times. You are reading books by women. But I say be wary. Things are sometimes reversed when you least expect it and I find myself, even now, in an awkward situation not unlike that of many women in old novels of chase and rescue.

Let me say first that the men in the valley and on the ridge across the way are not sheep ranchers at all, but cowboys and Spaniards in black hats, and they have tied me up in my own rope and taken my boots, though it's not as if I were some gorgeous blonde.

One of these independence days it'll be: Dear Tom: In Woman's Land the streets are paved with men: cowboys and motorcyclists, sailors and astronauts. Wait till you get here to make judgments. You'll see. It's really for the best.

But I forgot to mention that Jimmy came along, too, and on the long climb down he told me his life story, which was, I was surprised to hear, a lot like mine. His father had wanted baseball players while mine wanted champion swimmers. Jimmy was terrible. I was good, but not that good, and champion girls are not as fast as champion boys. Poor Daddy.

So we had crawled down the cliffs whispering together, we women bruising our breasts on outcroppings of rock, Jimmy thumping down on his balls. So we surprised them, but they outnumbered us twenty to one and they had guns, mountain tents, catalytic heaters, steaks and fried chicken, and I saw Tall and Dark walking among them as if he belonged there, not even winking at me. I think he knows both sides too well and can empathize with either one. I see that everybody's songs bring tears to his eyes. Still, he did follow me here, but what does that mean? And why did he let them tie me up when he knows I'd rather have fought to the death? I might have gotten my man even if they killed me.

John, John, will I ever again have your little arms around my neck? Your urine warm on my back that makes me feel like your real true-life mother? Will I hear you gurgle in my ear when I trip and catch myself in time? And will we ever walk hand in hand in Woman's Land? I think perhaps so, because my wrists are smaller than they expected or my clothesline stretches. I finally slip out of my bonds and step, in my socks, on the sharp, cold rocks, slipping away, melting into the darkness, I hope. But I don't go far before I bump into a silent, brooding man sitting apart from the others thinking about his life up to this time. Before I can hit him on the head with my dildo, he says, "I've been cheating on my wife and I've been cheating on my girl friend."

"First of all," I tell him, "that's not the way to put it. The very words you use imply a one-way view of things, but that you're thinking of it at all is a good sign in itself."

"It's so dark I can only see the gleam of his teeth.

"Are you Spanish?"

Just then the moon comes up and I see the handsome cowboy face. "Whoop ti eye are eye aye," repeated three times and "Git along, little dogie." (All this internal.)

"Once I meant to grow up to be a cowboy myself," I say (I loved horses and horse-faced men), "but, somehow, I forgot it or realized the utter futility, something of the sort. Anyway, I let my big dream die and hardly noticed that it had. Years have gone by since then."

"We all have our secret sorrows, but it's no life for a woman."

"There you go again." There he goes again. It's always that way.

"I'll be your cowboy," he says. "Then you won't have to be one yourself."

"Thanks," I say, "but I have a lot of mixed feelings about things like that." Then, just when he least expects it, I do hit him on the head with the dildo. I think I got my man, though, in a way, I'm a little sorry.

He did look Spanish.

There's just one trouble with trying to get away now. Already my feet hurt and there's blood on my socks. Where, oh, where is Tall and Dark to carry me back to the woman's camp in his arms?

And then I bump into another man, but it's really Jimmy trying to escape disguised as one of them. We're so glad to see each other we kiss and he lets out a squeal of delight and then we have to run for it. My feet are killing me, but after a few minutes of scrambling around, I see Tall and Dark in front of me and I jump into his arms.

Women! I got my man and I rode another one all the way back to our side of the cliffs, one noted for his leadership qualities, too. I could say that I, alone, am escaped to tell thee, except for Jimmy, Tall and Dark, Lil, Liz and Pat. Your darts have put a thousand men to sleep and it's dawn already, with the moon still up. Mother moon, we always say, or Big Ma in the sky. Gather up your bundles, Women. Spring is coming. Step out, and by tomorrow everything will be downhill.

Whistling, baby Johnny on my back (I hope he grows up to be six feet four and on our side), I cross the peak. Tomorrow we start down, but I don't expect it will be easy. That uses a whole new set of muscles.

74 75 76 77 10 9 8 7 6 5 4 3 2 1